HIDDEN ASSAILANT

Something slammed into the wooden siding on the front wall of the hotel, beside his ear, the sound like that of a heavy hammer slamming onto hard oak.

A heartbeat later the sound of that impact was followed by the dull bark of a gunshot.

Longarm dropped into a crouch and spun to face the threat. His Colt was in his hand already although he had no conscious recollection of drawing it.

Enough light remained from the late afternoon sun to show him a faint stream of white gunsmoke drifting away from the mouth of the alley across the street.

Longarm snapped a shot blindly into the alley, certain he would not hit anything but aware that not too many men will stand still when there are bullets coming toward them.

Another gunshot blasted out of the alley mouth, but this time the shooter was standing too far back inside the protection of the alley for Longarm even to see the smoke from his shot. The bullet thumped loud but harmless into the back of a rocking chair a good twenty feet away. It began to rock as if some unseen hand had tipped it back.

Longarm took the opportunity and charged straight at the alley mouth . . .

DON'T MISS THESE
ALL-ACTION WESTERN SERIES
FROM THE BERKLEY PUBLISHING GROUP

THE GUNSMITH by J. R. Roberts
Clint Adams was a legend among lawmen, outlaws, and ladies. They called him . . . the Gunsmith.

LONGARM by Tabor Evans
The popular long-running series about Deputy U.S. Marshal Long—his life, his loves, his fight for justice.

SLOCUM by Jake Logan
Today's longest-running action Western. John Slocum rides a deadly trail of hot blood and cold steel.

BUSHWHACKERS by B. J. Lanagan
An action-packed series by the creators of Longarm! The rousing adventures of the most brutal gang of cutthroats ever assembled—Quantrill's Raiders.

DIAMONDBACK by Guy Brewer
Dex Yancey is Diamondback, a southern gentleman turned con man when his brother cheats him out of the family fortune. Ladies love him. Gamblers hate him. But nobody pulls one over on Dex . . .

WILDGUN by Jack Hanson
Will Barlow's continuing search for his daughter, kidnapped by the Blackfeet Indians who slaughtered the rest of his family.

━━━ TABOR EVANS ━━━

LONGARM

ON THE BORDER

J

JOVE BOOKS, NEW YORK

This is a work of fiction. Names, characters, places, and incidents either are the product of the author's imagination or are used fictitiously, and any resemblance to actual persons, living or dead, business establishments, events, or locales is entirely coincidental.

LONGARM ON THE BORDER

A Jove Book / published by arrangement with
the author

PRINTING HISTORY
Jove edition / March 2002

Visit our website at
www.penguinputnam.com

ISBN: 0-515-13266-7

A JOVE BOOK®
Jove Books are published by The Berkley Publishing Group,
a division of Penguin Putnam Inc.,
375 Hudson Street, New York, New York 10014.
JOVE and the "J" design
are trademarks belonging to Penguin Putnam Inc.

PRINTED IN THE UNITED STATES OF AMERICA

10 9 8 7 6 5 4 3 2 1

Chapter 1

It was rare for Billy Vail to be late to work. Generally U.S. Marshal William Vail acted like he was in competition with his clerk, Henry, to see which of them would be first into the office, last out of it, and in general, the most efficient and productive worker not only in this office but in the whole of Denver's Federal Building.

This was a competitive event that Deputy Marshal Custis Long was not interested in joining, his own particular interests involving work only on occasion. Long, known by his friends and by a fair number of his enemies, too, as Longarm, was entirely content to sit in the marshal's Federal Building office waiting for the boss to show up.

Longarm sat relaxed in a ladderback chair with his legs crossed and an unlighted cheroot dangling from his lips. Henry had a bad cough and cigar smoke seemed to bother him, although he did not complain about it. Longarm figured he could wait to light up and concentrated instead on the morning's edition of the *Rocky Mountain News*.

Longarm was a tall man, lean in the hips and broad across the shoulders. He had dark brown hair and a massive handlebar mustache to match. His face was craggy, a deep tan setting off white teeth and lively brown eyes

1

that could register intelligence, humor or implacable enmity depending upon mood and situation.

He wore black stovepipe boots, brown corduroy trousers and a checked black and tan flannel shirt under a brown calfskin vest. A gold watch chain stretched between the vest pockets, and there was a large bore revolver riding in a crossdraw rig at his waist.

He had been one of Billy Vail's deputies for some years now and was generally regarded as being the best among them. And Billy Vail hired only the best to begin with. A man had to be good indeed to earn the marshal's trust.

Custis Long was the best. He had no ambitions to become the most diligent, too. "Dammit, Henry, if he don't show up by noon I'm going back to bed."

"I've never known you to be one to take naps," Henry said, looking up from the ever-present mountain of paperwork that graced his desk.

Longarm grinned at him. "I didn't say anything about sleeping. Nor being alone, if you'll recall." He liked Henry enormously. Moreover, he trusted him. Henry did not look much like a warrior with his mousy features and wire rim spectacles, but the clerk had sand in him and carried man-sized *cojones* hidden in his britches. But Henry was more than a little straitlaced and Longarm enjoyed scandalizing him now and then.

It was also perfectly true, though, that he had better things to do than sit around here waiting for the boss to show up. And the maid would be waking Gladys about eleven-thirty or so. If he left here at noon he should be there just about the time she finished her bath. They could have breakfast together—lunch for him, actually—and then see if they couldn't find some other way to amuse themselves on a snowy and miserable afternoon. Longarm suspected they would be able to think of something.

He plucked at one end of his watch chain and produced a key-wound Ingersol. It was past ten. And he could fudge that noon thing by half an hour or so. Whatever was keeping the boss, Longarm rather hoped it would continue. He folded the newspaper open to the page he'd been reading and laid the paper aside on a nearby chair, then stood and stretched.

"Want some coffee, Henry?" The clerks downstairs in the basement Records Department generally had hot coffee that they would share if they liked the fellow doing the asking. Upstairs in the offices frequented by the public, no coffee was allowed. Technically speaking, it wasn't allowed in Records either, but the boys there used a thin rubber hose to siphon gas away from the wall lamps for a ring burner that worked just fine.

The clerks in Records liked Longarm. He'd learned a long time ago that they were suckers for souvenirs brought back from his assignments, particularly any handiwork relating to the semi-tamed Indian tribes he sometimes dealt with. Longarm could not understand the fascination, but he was always willing to bring back some beaded moccasins or a parfleche pouch or perhaps a hank of wolf or coyote hair with some untanned skin attached— he never actually *said* these were scalps although the fellows in Records were allowed to make any assumptions they pleased. In exchange, they always had coffee available whenever he was in the office.

"No, thanks. But if you have a cure for the common cold let me know about it, will you?" Henry blew his nose, removed his glasses and used the same handkerchief to polish the lenses, then loudly sniffed.

"Rock and Rye is good for that," Longarm suggested.

Henry made a face. "Too sweet. I'll take bourbon, thank you."

"Got some rye in my flask. How about that?"

"You can buy me one after work. Not now. The boss wouldn't like it."

"The boss isn't here," Longarm reminded him.

3

"Want to bet on that?"

Longarm tilted his head. He could hear footsteps in the hallway, but surely Henry wouldn't be able to distinguish Billy Vail's steps from anybody else's.

A few seconds later, Longarm conceded that maybe Henry *could* tell Billy's footsteps from any others because the doorknob twisted just as the door was snatched rather angrily open and the marshal stepped inside.

"Good God, Billy, you look like a snowman," Longarm blurted.

It was the simple truth. The marshal was bundled to his ears in thick wool, including a muffler wrapped tight around his neck and a knitted woolen hat pulled over his ears and in front down to his eyebrows. And every visible inch of him looked like he'd been rolled in powdered sugar and then frozen. His clothing was covered with a rime of frost and snow and, close to his mouth where his breath touched the cloth, there were icicles too.

"Do . . . not . . . cross me . . . today," the normally affable marshal said in a slow and very tightly-controlled voice. "Do . . . not . . . fuck with me."

"Yes, sir," Longarm said respectfully. Henry said nothing at all and continued to keep his eyes fixed carefully on the papers before him.

"You!" the marshal declared, one finger aimed approximately between Longarm's eyes. "Come."

"Yes, sir."

Billy stormed into his private, inner office and Longarm meekly followed. There were damned few men Custis Long respected enough to defer to. Billy Vail was one of those few.

"Sit," the marshal ordered.

Longarm sat.

Billy Vail began shedding his garments, not even hanging them onto the rack in a corner of the office, but throw-

4

ing them haphazardly toward the base of the spindly wooden rack.

Longarm had no intention of saying or asking a damn thing, but Billy's murmured grumbling brought it out anyway. Overnight some mentally-impaired and decency-challenged juveniles had pulled a prank. They'd poured water onto the streetcar tracks on nearly an entire city block. When the water froze, which it did almost instantly in the intense cold Denver was currently experiencing, the streetcar horses could make no progress across the sheet of ice, despite caulks on their shoes. And if they had been able to go forward it would have done no good because the tracks themselves were iced solid so the passenger car wheels would have derailed.

"I'm going to catch those rotten little sons of bitches," Billy declared. "I'll lock them up. See if they think *that's* so funny. Sorry little bastards. They were standing there watching the driver try to get the car to move. I'm sure they are the same ones. They were laughing. *Laughing*, I tell you. I'll get them, Long. Mark my words, I'll have every one of them in jail."

To the best of Longarm's knowledge, pouring water onto a city street was not yet a federal crime. He rather doubted it fell under any state or county or city ordinances, either. But he did not think it politic to mention any of this to the marshal at this particular moment.

"And then, when the driver couldn't get the car to advance, he tried to telephone for a work crew to chip the ice away. Would you believe it? Ice had the telephone line down. He backed the car away. The last I saw him, he was still backing up. I had to walk to work. Couldn't find an available hansom cab. Every one I saw was in use. Not that I saw all that many out on the streets anyway. Lazy, good-for-nothing damned cab drivers. Didn't want to come out in the cold and help honest folk get on about their business. No, they stayed inside where it's nice and

5

warm, damn them. So I had to walk." He snorted. "Walk! Can you believe that?"

Which explained why the bald and normally ruddy marshal came in looking like a snowman with apples for cheeks. And some snot frozen onto his upper lip. Billy did not seem to be aware of that. Longarm decided against saying anything about it. Billy would find out soon enough. When it melted enough to drop off into Billy's lap. Longarm hoped he was present to see it when that happened. The expression on Billy's face at that moment would likely be a memory to cherish.

The marshal threw himself into the big swivel chair behind his desk and glared at Longarm so intently that Longarm was tempted to apologize. Or swear his innocence to . . . anything. Everything. Whatever.

"You!" Billy declared in an accusatory tone.

"Yes, sir?"

"I have to stay here in this miserable climate. You get to go south to where there is no winter, just blue skies and palm trees and handsome women. While I sit here freezing my butt off."

"I'm sure it will be tough, boss, but one of us has t' do it." For the first time since Billy walked in that door, Longarm began to openly smile. He found a sulfur tipped match in his pocket and flicked it aflame with his thumb nail so he could finally light the cheroot now that the smoke would not be a bother to Henry.

Chapter 2

Longarm checked the Ingersol again as he walked out of Billy's office with his instructions and all the proper documentation, vouchers, all that folderol folded and stuffed into the inside pocket of his sheepskin-lined winter coat. The time was 11:37 A.M. Longarm grinned. The timing could not have been better.

There was a cab standing at the end of the block, the driver waiting for another fare after presumably dropping someone else. It was just that kind of day, Longarm thought. For him, that is. Not for Billy Vail.

Longarm whistled. The horse pricked its ears first, then the hansom driver raised his head. He put the horse into a trot and quickly pulled to a halt in front of the Federal Building steps.

"Where to, mister?" The driver's teeth chattered and his lips were chapped and cracking. He had to need his income mighty badly to be out in weather like this. When they reached Longarm's destination he gave the driver three times a normal tip and hurried into the alley that ran beside the Sixteenth Street Opera House.

The backstage door was not locked. Longarm let himself in and stripped off his gloves. He kept his coat buttoned though. The stage and cavernous hall were not heated at this early hour.

"Who is ... oh, it's you, Marshal. I thought I heard somebody come in."

"Hello, Benny."

"You goin' upstairs, Marshal?"

Longarm laid a finger to his lips and winked at the janitor, then ran lightly up the stairs that led to the loft with all the tackle for handling curtains and props. At the back of the loft were three small but luxurious rooms, one for the exclusive use of the building's owner and the other two available for the stars who played here. Only one of the three was in use this month, the owner having quite sensibly gone south for the winter and only one headline act being booked at the moment. Longarm tapped lightly on the door of the one room that had a gilt star hanging in the place where a room number might otherwise have been found.

His knock was answered by an elfin, moon-faced little Oriental woman who might have been attractive if she hadn't had black teeth that were filed to sharp, fang-like points. Longarm always found Gladys's maid to be more than a little intimidating. He was afraid she might bite him.

"Is she awake, Chi?"

"She 'wake, suh. You come in." Chi stepped aside and once Longarm was in, slipped out, pulling the door closed behind her.

Longarm tiptoed into the inner room of the star's suite, dropping his hat and coat onto a settee as he went past.

Gladys was in the tub, humming softly to herself and scrubbing merrily away with a sponge and some perfumed soap. The tub was set facing the back wall, and Gladys could not see him without craning her neck around.

Longarm slipped up behind her and picked up another sponge from a tray set beside the copper-lined slipper tub.

8

He dipped it into the tepid bath water—there went any thoughts of joining Gladys in the tub, not in water that cool—and began lathering Gladys's back. She had a remarkably seductive back, he thought. Lean and trim. Very tidy. Longarm liked a good-looking back. The sight did something to him.

He scrubbed away for several moments, then reached around to lather—and to fondle—Gladys's breasts. The lady had a lean back but there was nothing spare about her tits. He let the sponge float away in the bathwater and began squeezing and kneading the abundant flesh there.

"Chi! Whatever are you . . . ?" Gladys turned her head. When she saw who it was who was making free with her body, she squealed. Then laughed. "When did you get here?"

"Half hour ago," he told her.

"Liar. I've only been in here a few minutes."

"You've been in long enough," Longarm said. "Now it's my turn to get in."

"You want to take a bath, dear?"

He leered at her. "It isn't the tub that I want to get into," he said. "Now stand up, will you, so I can sluice off these suds and get you dry."

"Custis, dear. I'm hungry!"

"That's all right. I can give you something to eat."

Gladys giggled. She held a hand out so he could help her to her feet. She lifted that magnificent body out of the soapy water, and Longarm took some time to admire what was on display before he used a pitcher of warm water to rinse her off, then handed her a towel.

Gladys Bolston was not bad to look at. Shapely legs. Narrow waist—she'd had a rib removed so she could turn what was small into something impossibly tiny when she was in costume—and of course those heavy tits. When she was an old woman those dugs would likely bounce

9

off her kneecaps when she walked. But she was young now, and her tits sagged only a little.

She had hair the color and gleam of a raven's wing, a complexion that might have been stolen from an ivory cameo, and the delicate facial features that would have been perfectly at home on a cameo brooch as well. Her eyes were a bright, startling blue.

And she had lips that were soft, mobile and *very* willing. Longarm explored her mouth with his own while Gladys was trying to dry herself off.

"Can't you wait until I'm done here?"

"No," he answered. He bent, scooped her up with one arm behind her back and the other behind her knees, and carried her still dripping to the huge, four-poster bed. The covers were still turned back as she'd recently gotten out of bed.

"Custis! I'm soapy."

"An' I'm horny."

"But I'm hungry. Really."

"First you take the edge off. Then we'll eat."

"You can have lunch with me? You aren't just going to have your fun and then leave?"

"I'm gonna be here this whole afternoon. Count on it." He had no particular train to catch. The man he needed to transport was already in custody. So why not?

Gladys shrieked with delight and flung her arms around his neck, getting his shirt wet. Which neither of them particularly minded.

Longarm reached the side of the bed, held her out over it and then dropped her onto it. Gladys laughed as she bounced up and down on the bedsprings.

The laughter died, though, when Longarm quickly unbuttoned his trousers and unleashed the monster that lived in there.

"Oh, sweetheart." Gladys reached out to fondle him.

10

Longarm knew what she liked. Soft and gentle love-making could come later. Right now. . . .

He shoved her legs apart and climbed onto the bed between them. He was still fully clothed, boots and gunbelt and all.

When he plunged inside her, the butt of his Colt gouged hard into the soft flesh of her belly. Gladys cried out and fiercely clutched at him with her arms and eager, grasping legs as well, holding him, forcing him deeper inside her body.

"Oh, baby, baby, baby," she moaned as her hips thrashed and her breath turned quickly ragged.

Longarm slammed into her belly over and over. He probably was hurting her. He knew to pay no attention to that.

He could feel Gladys's passion come to a rapid boil, her pussy wet and her movements frantic. He was going to have to take these trousers to the laundry right away for the cloth around the fly was surely soaked with Gladys's juices by now.

She cried out and convulsed beneath him, and Longarm felt his own sap rising.

Rising. Then exploding. Bursting beyond his ability to contain it and flowing into Gladys in a flood of heat and liquid pleasure.

Longarm collapsed onto Gladys, spent. For the moment. He buried his face into the side of her neck.

"Your mustache tickles," she said, her voice entirely calm and matter-of-fact, now that the moment of climax was past.

That was something that always amazed him. Gladys could be aroused in a heartbeat and climax almost as quickly. But then, once done, she was done.

For another, oh, five or ten minutes. At which point she would be ready to do it all over again.

The girl amazed him. But she also pleased him.

11

"Custis."

"Mmm?" He felt sleepy now. And warm. Definitely warm.

"Your gun is hurting me. And I'm hungry. Move, please. I'll have Chi bring something to eat. Do you like Chinese?"

"Yeah, but not Chi, thank you."

She slapped his shoulder. "She isn't Chinese. You know that."

"Yeah, but I thought it was funny."

"Well it wasn't. Now get up. And get undressed, will you?"

"I thought it usually worked the other way."

"Not this time. Do you want Chinese or not?"

"Not," he said. "Get me some Irish stew. And a bucket of beer. And some apple pan dowdy."

"God, you eat like a horse."

"All the better to have energy enough to keep up with you, m'dear."

She giggled. "In that case, I'll tell Chi to bring you a double order of stew." She shoved him off of her and walked naked into the front room. Longarm yawned and stretched, then stood and belatedly went about the task of getting out of his clothes. He was right though. There was pussy juice all over the front of his britches. Not that he was complaining.

He, too, was naked by the time Gladys returned to the bedroom. Apparently she'd had time enough to recover her interest now, for she gave him a remarkably lewd look and made an even more lewd suggestion.

Then she reached for him and dragged him—not unwilling—onto the rumpled bed.

The food, he knew, would be waiting for them by the time they were done with this second round of battle.

This was not at all a bad way to prepare for an assignment, Longarm decided, after giving the matter a good second or two of careful thought.

Chapter 3

Longarm's butt hurt. Five days of travel, all but one of it on bouncing, rattling, hard-sprung stage coaches, will do that to you. He would be more than pleased when the railroad was completed through Raton Pass and beyond. Then it should be possible to make it from Denver to El Paso in two easy days. In the meantime, a man had little choice but to suffer.

The coach rolled down one final, dusty street and came rocking to a halt in front of the stage offices. Longarm had spent the last half day seated on the roof rather than listen to the pissing and moaning of a thoroughly miserable old biddy who could not stand cigar smoke. He thanked the driver now and grabbed his own carpetbag off the roof rack.

"You! You there. I shall require my bags. Immediately, now. Move lively." It was the elderly cunt speaking. She was looking straight at him and snapping her fingers impatiently.

"No comprende," Longarm said, using up a very large percentage of his available Spanish. He had a few scattered words but no grasp of the grammar whatsoever.

The old bitch didn't bat an eyelash. She switched instantly to a fast and fluid Spanish, no doubt repeating her imperious request.

"Lady, I don't speak that neither."

"Oh!" She looked confused. Longarm took the opportunity to toss his saddle to the boards of the wooden sidewalk, then carried his carpetbag down after it. By the time he reached the ground, the old bag realized she'd been had and began to puff up like a toad.

"Young man, you can just climb right back up there and fetch down my things. And be careful with them or I shall . . . young man. Young *man*! You come back here this instant."

Longarm picked up his things and walked away, a cheroot clamped firmly between his teeth. He regretted now that he'd left the relative comfort of the coach interior. If he had to do it over again he'd stay. And smoke his cheroots one after another until the old bitch turned blue.

"Hello, Marshal. It's a pleasure to see you again," was the greeting he received at the Conquistadore Hotel a few blocks away. "Would you care for the same room you had before?"

Incredible. He hadn't been here in . . . what? two years or a little more. He felt thoroughly ashamed of himself that he couldn't remember the clerk's name. "That would be fine, thanks."

"My pleasure, Marshal." The man spun the guest register around to face him, then turned around to fetch a key down from a rack of them beside the message pigeonholes. "Number twenty-seven," he said as he laid the key beside the register. "You know where it is."

"Yes, thank you."

The desk clerk snapped his fingers and a Mexican boy of twelve or thirteen came at a trot from somewhere in the dining area.

John! That was the clerk's name. John . . . he still couldn't recall the last name though. "Thank you, John."

14

The clerk beamed in response to Longarm's use of his name.

Longarm let the bellboy take his things. John gave the boy instructions in Spanish. Probably telling him the room number, Longarm assumed.

"D'you speak English, son?" Longarm asked on their way upstairs, heading toward the back of the hotel.

"Si, senor." And who could argue with an answer like that? Longarm concluded. The boy carried the carpetbag and saddle inside the room and put the saddle discretely away in the bottom of the wardrobe, then placed the carpetbag on a luggage rack and began fumbling with the straps to open it.

"That's all right, son. I can do the unpacking, thank you."

The boy went right on with what he was doing. Yeah, he spoke English just fine, Longarm thought. "Whoa. That's good. That's enough." The boy looked up and Longarm gave him a smile and held his hand up, palm outward to tell him to stop. Longarm gave him a tip and got a heartfelt *gracias* in return. That was fine. It was another word on the short list of ones that Longarm understood.

Longarm saw the bellboy out and bolted the door behind him, then went to tend to his unpacking. Not that there was so much involved. He did not expect to be here very long and was traveling light. He'd left his Winchester at home for one thing. It wasn't a good idea to carry too much luggage or firearms when there was a prisoner to transport. He'd considered leaving the saddle behind as well but eventually decided against that, more out of force of habit than any genuine expectation that it might be needed.

He put his things away, then rang downstairs for bath water. Travel by coach on New Mexico's roads was a dusty prospect, and Longarm hadn't had a chance to bathe since he left Denver. He felt gritty and grimy.

The same boy brought the water and wrestled the tub into the room. Longarm tipped him again and had to shoo him away again once the bath was ready. *"Gracias, senor."* Still not a word of English from him.

Longarm felt considerably better once he'd had his bath and was dressed in fresh underwear and a clean shirt. He balled his soiled things together and rang for the kid again.

It was late in the day by then. Too late to be thinking about the prisoner. He could keep until tomorrow. Right then Longarm was more interested in doing something about the empty feeling in his belly. And he just might talk himself into having a sip of something to drink afterward.

Chapter 4

Longarm checked the Regulator wall clock in the lobby as he headed for the street. He decided that it was probably too early to catch the El Paso night marshal on duty but it couldn't hurt to swing past city hall just to see. Assuming, that is, his old friend was still night marshal. By now, Carlton might've decided to hang up his gunbelt in favor of a rocking chair and a long-haired *senorita* to act as his nursemaid. And wouldn't Doreen let him get away with that. The thought was enough to make Longarm smile. Carlton and Doreen had been married approximately forever and were as well matched as any two people Longarm ever knew.

He made his way around to the back of the massive public building and walked into the police station by way of a separate entrance where the townspeople could seek assistance day or night.

Longarm was mildly disappointed to see that his friend was not behind the large desk that was positioned to face the door. The desk was occupied instead by a different man, presumably an officer, although he was not wearing one of the city's baggy blue uniforms. The man was about Longarm's age, but the resemblance ended there—or at least Longarm hoped it did—for this man was . . . greasy.

Longarm cocked his head to one side and contemplated the fellow for a moment, trying to decide what it was about the officer that he did not like. There was nothing he could put a finger on, nothing that actually stood out. But if he'd been a local officer himself, he would have put the roust on this one. Shake him down, shake him up and run his presumed-innocent ass right out of town. Preventative law enforcement, Longarm believed, had its place.

Not that this fellow was his to worry about. Fortunately.

"What're you staring at, mister?" the officer demanded. His tone of voice was about as welcoming as the whir of a rattlesnake's tail.

Longarm was actually rather pleased to see that attitude on display. It would have been a pity to take such an instant dislike to a man and then discover that he was a pleasant fellow after all.

Despite his gut reaction, though, Longarm's voice was calm and polite. "I'm looking for Carlton Mitchell," he said mildly.

"You don't need him. Whatever you want, I can handle it."

"I doubt that," Longarm said. "I want. . . ."

"I don't give a shit what you want, asshole," the officer interrupted. "I'm on duty here, not that old fart."

"I see," Longarm said. He was smiling as he approached the broad desk that was set onto a six-inch-high platform so it would allow the desk officer to look down at the folks who came before him. A little physical intimidation like that sometimes helped forestall trouble, and God knew any small scrap of assistance was worth reaching for when you had to deal with the sort of people who came under a lawman's scrutiny.

He was still smiling when he reached across that desk, took a firm hold on the officer's shirt collar and pulled him closer until they were nose to nose. The officer had eaten something with onions in it not too long ago, and his breath could have used some help.

"Hey, dammit!" The officer grabbed for his gun. It was a move Longarm anticipated, and Longarm got there first. He took the officer's hand in his with the little finger separated from the others, then squeezed, bending the finger back toward the wrist. He didn't break the finger. Quite. But it had to hurt like hell.

Longarm's smile did not fade when he gently asked, "Could you please tell me where I can find Marshal Mitchell?"

"I don't . . . I didn't . . . jeez, mister. I didn't mean nothing. You know?"

"What I know," Longarm said with exaggerated patience, "is that I am tired and I am hungry and I would like to speak with an old friend. You are not my friend and I don't think you are fixing to become one. Now, I will ask you one more time . . ." He very slightly increased the pressure on that finger. "Do you happen to know where I can find Carlton?"

"Jesus, mister, I . . ."

"You can call me Marshal, not mister. Deputy United States Marshal Long. My friends call me Longarm. I do not want you to call me Longarm. Am I making myself clear?"

"Yes, I . . . I mean, yes *Marshal.*"

Longarm let go of his hand and released his hold on the shirt too. But kept an eye on the hand, lest the fellow decide to go for that belly gun again. He did not. Instead he slumped into the swivel chair and leaned back as far as he could, placing himself out of Longarm's reach.

"I didn't mean nothing, mis—Marshal. Really," the fellow said.

"Of course you didn't. Let's say we got off to a bad start and let it go at that, shall we?"

"Yeah, sure. We'll do that, Marshal."

Not that the officer meant a word of it, of course. But that was fair enough. Longarm didn't mean it either.

"Now, could you please tell me where I can find Carlton?"

"He's at the cemetery," the desk officer said.

"Oh, damn!"

"No, no, it isn't him that's dead; it's his wife."

"Oh, Jesus," Longarm blurted.

"He goes to the cemetery first thing every afternoon when he wakes up. Then he gets something to eat before he comes on duty."

"Doreen. What happened to her?"

"Came down sick with something. An epizootic of some kind. A lot of people had it, but not too many died of it. This was, oh, a couple months ago, I think. Mitchell's wife went fast, they said. Two, three days an' she was gone. It hit the old man pretty hard."

It would, Longarm knew. Carlton adored Doreen. Losing her was sure to have been rough on him.

"Thank you for the information." He nodded and turned his back on the officer.

If he'd been pressed on the point, though, he would have had to admit that his ears were straining to hear any sound from behind that desk indicating the desk officer—who never bothered to give his name—wanted to provoke Longarm now that he wasn't looking.

As it happened, the man lacked either the inclination or the guts, and Longarm walked out of the police station without further incident.

Chapter 5

Longarm had no idea where the cemetery might be. But he figured he knew who would. He found a cab and climbed inside. "How much to the cemetery?" he called to the driver on the box above.

"Thirty-five cents one way, fifty cents round trip. Extra if I have to wait more than a half hour."

Longarm had no way to know if the price was reasonable or not since he did not know how far the destination might be. "Let's go." He took out a cheroot and lighted it.

The cheroot was not half smoked by the time the cab rolled to a halt again and the driver called down, "Here you go, mister. Should I wait?"

Longarm stepped down and took a look around before he answered. If Carlton came out here on horseback, Longarm would want the cab again. There were no saddle horses in sight, but parked nearby was a light buggy with a folding top and a shaggy brown horse standing hipshot while it chewed on the contents of a canvas feedbag affixed to its bridle.

"No need t' wait," Longarm said. He paid the man forty

cents and let himself in through the wrought iron fence that surrounded the cemetery.

He found his friend seated on a bench beside a small clump of cedars. Carlton did not look good. He had lost weight since Longarm saw him last and he was in need of a haircut and a shave. His clothing looked like he rarely bothered to change, and two buttons were missing on the vest that hung loose on his newly gaunt frame.

Carlton Mitchell used to be a large, vigorous, happy man. He was none of those things now. The impression Longarm got was that somehow he'd shrunk. But then it was no surprise that he would be taking Doreen's death mighty hard.

Carlton barely looked up when Longarm approached and helped himself to a seat on the bench beside him.

" 'H'lo, Longarm." His voice was matter-of-fact and without enthusiasm, although it had been two years, give or take a little, since they last saw each other. There was no welcoming smile. His expression was dour.

"Hello, Carlton."

"You found me here so I expect you've already heard."

"Uh."

"Twelfth day of June. Ten-twenty in the morning. I was holding her hand. She just . . . slipped away from me. You know?"

"I'm sorry," Longarm said. There was a strong scent of whiskey on Carlton's breath.

"Yeah. Everybody's fucking sorry. Doesn't do a thing to bring her back, does it?" There was bitterness in his voice.

"Nothing will do that," Longarm said.

"No. Nothing will." He pulled a flask from his pocket and offered it. Longarm shook his head. He would have enjoyed a drink, actually. But he didn't want to encourage Carlton to have any more. Longarm hoped if he refused, Carlton would put the cap back on the flask and put it away. He didn't. He shrugged and took a long pull at the silver flask, then another before he put it away.

"Doreen hated whiskey," Longarm said. "Remember how she'd fuss when you and me would go out to tip a few?"

"Shut the fuck up, Custis. You're being too obvious. If you got something to say, come right out and say it."

Longarm thought about that for a moment, then said, "You already know what people think, so what's the point?"

"No point at all. I'm free, white and way the hell over twenty-one. I'll do as I damn please."

Longarm nodded. "Fair enough."

"What are you here for this time?"

Longarm told him.

"You need any help?"

"If you'd care to go across the border with me it might do me some good. They're likely t' know you over there."

"Extradition." Mitchell mouthed the word slowly, as if tasting it. He made a face. "Heard about it. Don't think I've ever seen it before though. Oh, we sometimes make little swaps back and forth across the border. But as a courtesy, not with actual papers. No sir, don't think I've ever seen an actual extradition before now."

"They aren't common," Longarm agreed.

"Any idea why the Meskins agreed to it this time instead of taking a little payoff and looking the other way?"

"I wondered the same thing," Longarm admitted. "My boss Billy Vail—you remember him—"

"Hell, I knew Billy when he was a Texas Ranger. He's one salty son of a bitch. Doesn't look it worth a damn, but don't ever get into a showdown with him. Not for serious. He knows what powder smoke smells like."

"Uh huh. Anyway, what Billy thinks is that it's political. Theirs, not ours. Somebody down there wants Jurneman out of their hair. No idea why they don't toss him

23

in one of their own jails or stand him in front of a firing squad. No idea why he was arrested down there to start with. But whatever it is, they don't want to handle it themselves. Billy thinks it's more convenient for them if we take him out of circulation."

"Jurneman," Mitchell repeated. He thought for a moment, then shook his head. "No, I've never heard of him."

"Would you have?"

"Maybe. Maybe not. Depends what he's done. If he'd robbed somebody over on the Del Norte side or shot up a bar or killed somebody, yeah I'd've heard about that, pretty certain. But if he did something down in the interior or got crossways with the dons, no I probably wouldn't. We exchange information on the routine stuff, Longarm, but you couldn't say that us and the Meskins are buddy-buddy. What'd the guy do on this side of the river anyhow?"

"Murder."

"That's no federal crime," Mitchell said. "What brings you into it?"

"It was a postal worker he killed. Young guy, a clerk, riding in the mail car on a Central and Southern train. It happened in our district, so that makes it our jurisdiction and our prosecution. I'll fetch him back, then they'll try him in Denver and likely hang him over at Leavenworth. Or give him a long sentence, then turn him over to the state for another trial under Colorado law and then let them hang him. It depends on politics and whose prosecutors need to take credit. The good thing is, I don't have to care about any of that. All I have to do is sign the paper and take him home in irons. Piece of cake."

Mitchell snorted. "I grew up along this border, Longarm, and spent most all my life carrying a badge inside spitting distance of the Rio Grande. I've never yet seen anything be a 'piece of cake' when it comes to something between them and us."

"Yeah, well, this time maybe it will be different." Longarm stood. "You want to show me where Doreen is, old friend? I'm kinda rusty when it comes to talking to the Big Boss, but I'd like to say something anyhow. Then maybe you'll give me a ride back to town. I just got in around mid-day and haven't had anything but a stale doughnut since morning."

Cartilage snapped loud enough for Longarm to hear when Carlton stood. "Right over here," he said, leading the way to a low mound that was very carefully raked and tended.

Chapter 6

Longarm had supper. Steak, fried potatoes—an ordinary meal. Carlton had a water tumbler full of whiskey. Longarm grimaced but said nothing. There would have been no point. If a man was damn well determined to drink himself to death, it didn't matter whether his friends liked it or not.

"Mighty big steak they gave me," Longarm said at one point. "Be a shame to waste any of it. How 'bout you help me out with some? I could get the waiter to bring another plate."

Carlton's only response was a dirty look.

"You still working nights?" Longarm asked.

The aging widower nodded. "Same as always."

"Get off about daybreak?"

"That's right."

"How about you get some sleep, then come by the hotel an' we'll go across together. It'd be a help."

"I don't sleep much these days, Longarm. I'll just come by soon as I'm relieved. Which hotel?"

Longarm told him, and soon after the El Paso night marshal finished his whiskey and stood. "I better be going now. Go relieve that son of a bitch Worrell."

"That's the guy on the desk?" Longarm asked.

Mitchell nodded.

"I take it you don't like him."

"My friend, nobody likes Sergeant Worrell. Except for the chief, that is. Worrell is his brother-in-law. I'll see you in the morning." Carlton came very near to smiling for a moment. "If you can still get up in the morning."

"Is it getting out of bed you're talking about, or . . . ?"

Carlton Mitchell grunted, then turned and made his way through the maze of tables in the cafe and out into the waning daylight. His step was firm and sure, and if Longarm hadn't known Carlton was drinking, he would not have seen it reflected in his friend's movement.

Longarm shook his head, then returned to his steak and spuds.

El Paso was not exactly a cosmopolitan city, despite its size and the fact that it was located on one of the major east-west routes of travel within the United States. And that was saying nothing about the north and south traffic that still ran between Old and New Mexico.

Not that Longarm would normally give a shit. But, dammit, he never had found a source in El Paso for the Maryland distilled rye whiskey that he enjoyed. The closest he could come here was rye made in Pennsylvania. It wasn't bad, mind. But it wasn't the smooth and flavorful Maryland rye either.

Sometimes, he reflected over a glass of the Pennsylvania product, a man has to make sacrifices in the name of duty.

"Another?" the barman offered.

"Sure." Longarm accepted the refill and the bartender dragged a dime out of the loose change lying on the bar. That was decent of him. Whiskey was two shots for a quarter or fifteen cents for one. Since Longarm ordered only one to begin with, the barman would have been en-

27

tirely justified to expect fifteen cents for each drink. Classy, Longarm thought. Not cosmopolitan perhaps. But that was definitely classy. And hell, the Pennsylvania rye was really pretty decent. Considering.

"Help yourself to the free lunch, friend," the bartender said.

"Thanks, but I'm full. This right here is all I'll be needing." Longarm saluted the gent with his glass, then took a swallow and dug into his pocket for a cheroot.

"Move your ass, lardbutt."

Longarm looked toward the far end of the bar. The voice was familiar. So was the man behind it. It seemed that Sergeant Worrell was off duty and bent on a little recreation. This time he had decided to torment a fat man in a black broadcloth suit and a derby hat that had seen better days.

"Sorry," the fat man said and moved aside to make room at the bar.

Worrell pushed his way to the bar, then deliberately shouldered the fat man. Hard. "I said move your ass. Now *move* it!"

"You have plenty of room, mister," the fat man protested.

"Don't back talk me."

The fat man looked like he'd had just about enough of Worrell. "Go fuck yourself." He turned his back to Worrell and picked up the beer he'd been enjoying before the police sergeant arrived.

Worrell turned red as a new bandanna. The bartender saw what was happening and hurried toward the two, but he was too far away to stop Worrell from raising his belly gun and delivering a crunching blow to the back of the head of the unsuspecting fat man.

The fat man's eyes rolled back in his head and he dropped to the floor like a poleaxed shoat, sprawling face forward into the sawdust and damn near tipping over a cuspidor in the process.

"Dammit, Ronny, you didn't have to do that," the barkeep protested.

"Shut your mouth, George, or I'll take a little stroll into your back room looking for violations of the health code. Now don't just stand there. Give me a beer. Put it on my tab."

Longarm wondered if that tab was ever paid. Not that it was any of his business, of course. He drained off the last of the Pennsylvania rye and ambled down the length of the bar toward Sergeant Worrell and the groggy fat man, who was just then beginning to groan and stir.

Worrell saw him coming and glowered. "I don't need your help," he said.

Longarm smiled thinly, the expression not reaching his eyes at all. "T'wasn't you I thought I'd help."

"Don't interfere with me, federal man. I'm making a legitimate arrest here. It's got nothing to do with you."

"Really? What's the charge?"

"None of your fucking business, that's what the charge is."

"Uh huh." Longarm bent and took the fat man under the armpits and helped him onto his feet, propping him against the bar and pulling the fellow's beer close to hand.

"I told you, dammit, that back talking son of a bitch is my prisoner. I'm taking him in. And if you stick your nose into it, I'll arrest you, too. You want to know the charge? Interfering with a police officer in the performance of his duty. And don't think your federal badge will get you out of it. You'll get ten days and no bail if I decide to take you in."

Longarm smiled at him again, then returned his attention to the fat man. Longarm picked up the derby, pushed it back into shape where the butt of Worrell's .455 Webley crushed it and checked to make sure there was no open wound on the back of the man's head before he set the hat gently onto the fellow's head again. "Sorry, mister. I wasn't close enough to keep him from hitting you."

The fat man gave Longarm a brief stricken look, his attention focused mainly on Worrell. "You can't arrest me. I haven't done anything," he bleated.

"He isn't arresting you, friend. Don't worry about it," Longarm assured him.

"I *told* you, asshole, keep out of this."

"Tsk, tsk," Longarm clucked. "Such language. Your mother would be ashamed of you." Longarm paused for a moment as if in reflection, then asked, "By the way. Do you happen to know who she is?"

Worrell let out a roar and once again grabbed for his revolver. Longarm did not bother with his own Colt. He simply chopped the edge of his hand, hard, onto Worrell's wrist as the Webley cleared leather for the second time in as many minutes. The heavy gun spun out of Worrell's grasp and onto the floor, causing most of the nearby spectators to do a quick little dance as they hurried to get the hell out of the way.

Sergeant Worrell had been angry before? That was but a pale prelude to the rage that filled him now. His face turned purple with fury, and he balled his fists and ducked his chin close to his chest.

"You son of a *bitch*!"

Worrell began shuffling forward in a prize fighter's crouch, both forearms lifted and fists cocked.

Chapter 7

Longarm quickly backpedaled away from the furious police sergeant. The fellow did not seem entirely in his right mind. That didn't bother Longarm particularly. But it did disturb him a bit that, in addition to being so unnecessarily belligerent, Worrell looked and acted like he'd had some formal training in the manly art of pugilism.

Longarm too raised his fists in the approved Marquis of Queensbury manner. He was both familiar and comfortable with the style if not exactly schooled in it as Worrell seemed to be.

Longarm was good. He was not particularly foolish. And he hadn't come all this way just to have his face and hands chopped up by some idiot who possessed neither restraint nor common sense.

Better not to take any chances with him, Longarm concluded while Worrell was busy hurling accusations.

"Stand and fight, you yellow son of a bitch," the sergeant was shouting. He added a number of other choice phrases that Longarm ignored, while continuing to back away from Worrell's bull-like advance.

Longarm waited until the distance and the footwork seemed appropriate.

Then he stepped forward and planted the toe of his right boot into Sergeant Worrell's gonads. Hard.

A gasp rose from the crowd who'd gathered close in anticipation of a free boxing match.

Something closer to a sigh escaped Worrell's lips as the sergeant turned instantly and completely pale, white as the proverbial ghost. He seemed to be in too much pain to be interested in screaming.

At least in that first moment of shock.

Then the pain reached him and he let out a howl that would have made a steam engine proud.

Worrell bent over to clutch himself and collapsed in a heap on the saloon floor, writhing and squirming there. Tears began to stream out of his eyes and mucous from his nose, the snot trickling unnoticed into his mouth, which was gaping open like a trout thrown onto a creek bank.

Longarm considered the officer's current state and concluded that Ronny Worrell very likely had had enough for one evening's entertainment. Longarm returned to his place at the bar. The remainder of his change, dammit, had disappeared while his attention was diverted. He dug a quarter out of his pocket and laid it on the bar. "One more, please."

"It's on the house, friend," the bartender said. "But if I was you, mister, I'd be gone from here before daybreak. Ronny isn't one to forgive nor forget. He'll come after you, and you should know that he's kin to the county judge."

Longarm smiled and accepted the rye that was placed before him. "Thanks, but I expect my Uncle Sam can trump his judge."

"Yeah? You got powerful kin here too, eh?"

"So t' speak," Longarm said, with something of a twinkle in his eye.

He savored a swallow of the Pennsylvania rye, then

tossed back the rest and thanked the bartender for both the drink and the advice. Then he winked at the fat man down at the far end of the bar and walked out past Sergeant Worrell, who was only then beginning to become aware that there was a world outside the limits of his own bruised and battered stones.

Ronny-boy would be hurting when he pissed for the next week, Longarm figured.

Couldn't happen to a nicer fellow.

Longarm ambled back to his hotel, unconcerned about who or what might be behind him.

Chapter 8

When Carlton Mitchell hadn't shown up by nine o'clock, Longarm quit waiting in the hotel lobby and went looking for him. Carlton was seated behind the big desk where the duty sergeant normally presided.

"Sorry, Longarm, but that damned lazy Worrell didn't show up for work this morning. The chief asked me to wait until he can find another officer who *thought* he was going to have the day off today."

Longarm grinned. "It wasn't laziness that kept the good sergeant away this morning."

Carlton raised an eyebrow, so Longarm explained what happened the evening before. "It may be a day or two before he feels up to working again," Longarm said. "You might want to warn your chief to make other arrangements." Longarm's grin got bigger.

Mitchell laughed. "I suppose I should be upset that one of our people is hurt. Funny thing. I just can't manage it."

"Neither could the other men in the saloon," Longarm noted. "Popular fella, your Ronny Worrell."

"Yes, isn't he? But if I were you, Longarm, I'd watch my back once he gets on his feet again. He thinks he can get away with anything in this town. And hell, maybe he can. So you might want to be careful."

"I'll prob'ly have my prisoner and be on my way back to Denver before nightfall tonight," Longarm said.

"Not if you have to wait on me before you go collect him," Mitchell said. "I know how our guys are about working when they're scheduled to have an off day. I could be stuck here all day long."

"Are you all right, Carlton?"

"Just fine, thanks."

Actually he did look better this morning than he had the evening before. And if he'd been drinking through the night, it certainly did not show now. But then Carlton took duty seriously. It could be that he did not drink when he was on the job. If so, then the more time Carlton spent behind that desk or walking the alleys at night, the better.

"I'd've liked both your company and your help, Carlton, but I reckon I'll go on over an' get my prisoner."

"Will you stop by again before you leave?"

"Sure. If it's late by the time I get him to this side of the border I'll stick him in your lock-up until morning. If things go smoothly, I'll drop by to say good-bye at the least. There's a coach going north about four this afternoon if I remember a'right. I'd like to be on it if I can." Longarm winked. "Got something interesting to look forward to in Denver if I get back before the troupe moves on again."

"Actress?"

"Singer," Longarm told him.

"Pretty?"

Longarm rolled his eyes and used his hands to sketch an hourglass shape in the air.

"I've been . . ." Carlton thought better of what he intended to say and just shook his head instead.

Longarm's expression turned serious for a moment.

35

"You know, old friend, it's all right for you t' be horny. It's natural for a man."

"But Doreen..." Mitchell clamped his jaw closed again.

"She'd understand, Carlton. I bet you never strayed a minute the whole time you two was married."

"Of course not!" Mitchell retorted. He sounded offended by the mere idea of cheating on the woman he'd loved so deeply.

"Carlton. You ain't married now. It's all right if you get you some dark-eyed little gal t' come in an' warm your bed as well as make it up. It's okay."

"I don't—I can tell you one thing, Longarm. It makes me feel like shit to be whacking off at my age." He reached up and rumpled the crest of pale gray hair that crowned his head.

Longarm couldn't help but laugh at the idea of Carlton Mitchell sneaking off to the backhouse with the intention of pounding the old pud. The visual image of it was ludicrous.

"Get you one o' those pretty little Meskin girls, Carlton. Pick you a shapely one about fifteen years old with hair down to her butt and more energy than you or me can remember ever having. Let her drain you dry a few times an' you'll see how much better it makes you feel."

"Go away, Longarm. Your sort of advice is bad for an old fart like me."

"Nope. Do what I say an' see if you don't feel better for it."

"Get outa here, Custis."

"Want me to bring you back a cute one?"

Mitchell wadded a scrap of paper into a ball and threw it at Longarm. Longarm laughed and headed outside.

With luck he could make that stage and be home well before Gladys and her bunch moved on to Virginia City.

Chapter 9

He was in luck. There was a bridge across the Rio Grande linking the two halves of El Paso del Norte, the Pass of the North.

Both cities, the American and the Mexican, were officially known by that name, but in common usage the American side was called El Paso and the southern Mexican side Del Norte. It eliminated a lot of confusion.

There frequently was confusion, though, about the many bridges that were built between the two. Often the spring flooding on the river would tear away man's best efforts, sweeping the scraps and splinters that had been a bridge downriver toward Del Rio, Laredo, Brownsville and the Gulf of Mexico. It didn't happen every year, but when it did there was often acrimony between the American and Mexican officials about who was to pay what to whom, the result being that it could take a while before a new bridge was constructed.

Today, fortunately, there was a sturdy bridge in place and Longarm joined the stream of traffic. Pedestrians by the hundreds squeezed along both sides of the bridge while heavily-laden freight wagons and gaudily painted hacks competed for space in the middle. The border was loud, chaotic and alive with energy. Longarm loved it.

He made his way through the madness and found a uniformed officer on the south side. Longarm had no idea if the man was police or military or from some other agency, but at least he represented the Mexican government in one capacity or another.

"City hall?" Longarm asked. He stopped and tried to work out how to ask the question in Spanish. City was *ciudad*. He was sure of that. But hall? If he'd ever heard the word, it eluded him now.

The Mexican, in his pale tan uniform and highly polished Sam Browne belt, smiled, and gave Longarm directions in perfect English.

"Thank you," Longarm said, "uh, *gracias*." He was sure of that one too.

"It is too far to walk," the soldier/cop/whatever said and hailed a passing *carreta*. He then gave the driver instructions in a torrent of Spanish and helped Longarm onto the high-wheeled, red, yellow and green vehicle.

Two minutes later, the carreta stopped. It was not exactly too far to walk, but in fairness to that fellow in the uniform—with or without the language question—it was probably easier to give directions to someone who knew the city than to a stranger like Longarm.

Longarm was deposited in front of a handsome two-story building with palm trees planted inside the adobe wall that surrounded it.

Palm trees. And warm weather at this time of year. Longarm wondered if the U.S. marshal for this district needed another deputy.

He paid the driver and entered the Del Norte city hall.

"Of course, *senor*. We expect you." The captain—he was a soldier not a cop, but then, down here the two sometimes seemed interchangeable, in Longarm's view— smiled and held out his hand.

For a moment Longarm thought he was brazenly requesting a bribe. What they called *mordida* down here.

"You have the necessary papers, *senor?*"

Longarm dug through his inside coat pocket, pulling out tri-folded sheets of paper and opening them one by one. Travel authorization. Claim for expenses. Warrant ready for service on Adolph Jureman . . . Ah! Request for Extradition. That was the one he wanted now. He replaced the rest in his pocket and handed the extradition request to the Mexican officer. The paper carried the signatures of the United States Attorney General, the Denver district chief judge and the Mexican ambassador. It must have taken a considerable amount of time to procure, having to travel back and forth across half a continent in order to secure all the signatures that were required.

"Very good, *senor*. Everything seems to be in order." The Mexican—his name was Ignacio Fernandez—smiled again, and produced a canvas-bound ledger from a lower desk drawer and made a notation in it. He selected a rubber stamp from another drawer, carefully inked it with red ink, and with a flourish stabbed the bottom of the extradition request with it. He wiped the stamp free of ink and returned it to the drawer where it belonged. Then he found pen and ink—already prepared, thank goodness— and scrawled yet another signature onto the form, this time in the red area that he'd just created with his stamp.

Whatever would bureaucrats do without rubber stamps and red ink? Longarm wondered as he stood silently watching this laborious process.

"Excellent," Captain Fernandez said at length. He smiled up at Longarm.

"May I take my prisoner now, please?"

Fernandez looked quite thoroughly stricken by that insane notion. "Take him now? But, *senor* . . . the authorization. We must first procure the authorizations, no?"

"I thought . . ." Longarm, pointed to the paperwork ly-

39

ing all nicely signed and stamped in the center of the captain's desk.

"Oh, no, *senor*. There are forms to complete. Signatures must be obtained. Oh, no. So much still to do, eh? But do not worry yourself. I personally will take this matter in my charge. We will get done all that must be done." He smiled. "Trust this to me, *senor*."

Longarm began to get a wee sense of uneasiness. But he managed a smile. "Of course, Captain. Thank you."

Fernandez pulled a bulbous watch—silver, not gold—from a vest pocket and consulted it. "Immediately after dinner and siesta, *senor*. I will begin immediately then, yes."

"D'you think I can have him and be on my way this afternoon then?" Silly question. Longarm was afraid he already knew the answer.

"Oh no, *senor*. That would not be possible, I think. *Mañana*, maybe so."

Mañana. That too was a word Longarm knew. Didn't like it. But he certainly knew what it meant.

They claimed that it was the Spanish word for "tomorrow." They lied. *Mañana*, he was convinced, properly translated to "possibly someday or perhaps not at all." *Mañana*, indeed.

Captain Fernandez smiled.

Chapter 10

There was no point to hanging around the Del Norte city hall all day waiting for Captain Fernandez to have his lunch and his nap and then—maybe—get around to doing some work on the extradition. Indeed, the captain seemed more than a little relieved when Longarm excused himself and said he would call again tomorrow. Early. Ready to sign for Jurneman and take the next coach north.

"Very good, *senor*. I shall do all that I can to arrange this." He smiled. "Trust me."

Yeah, right. "I do, captain. Thank you." Managed to say it with a straight face, too. He was rather proud of himself for that.

It was not yet mid-day and already the sun was hot. In Denver they were probably huddling around the stoves, coughing from the usual winter combination of head colds and coal smoke. Longarm decided he preferred palm trees to icy sidewalks any day of the week.

A short line of *carretas* waited outside city hall, but Longarm didn't even think about hiring one. He hadn't known where he was going before, but in order to find the border again all he had to do was head north. He would know he was there when his feet got wet.

Whistling a cheerful ditty from Gladys's repertoire, he started north at a leisurely pace.

A street vendor selling tamales attracted his attention, so he stopped there. The middle-aged salesman had no English and Longarm no real Spanish, but American money was as acceptable on this side of the border as those big, silver pesos were on the El Paso side. About all the language that was really needed was the ability to point and to show a palm full of coins.

Longarm bought a tamale. Tried it. Bought another. He smiled and gave the vendor a hearty *gracias* before walking on.

In the next block there was another vendor, this one swelling *sopapillas*. They were mighty good too.

So were the tortillas wrapped around refritos. And a chili relleno. And a sugar-coated chocolate confection. And. . . .

By the time Longarm reached the main street that ran south from the border bridge, he had no further need for lunch. He was so full, he was groaning. Didn't regret a single mouthful, but he didn't want any more for a while either.

What he did want was something to drink. That was a need that could be quite readily filled in Del Norte. A good third of the businesses on the principal street seemed to be saloons of one sort or another. Big and small ones. Quiet and noisy ones. Saloons filled with laughter and saloons where the sounds of fistfights drifted through the doorways.

Longarm found a large but quiet saloon on a street corner and peeked inside. The interior was cool and shady. Stools were lined up along the bar instead of having the usual rail where a gentleman could prop himself up while he drank. More than half of the stools were occupied. And more than half of the patrons were female. Mighty pretty females at that. Apparently a gent could find more here than a beer or a shot of tequilla.

On an impulse, Longarm stepped inside and found a trio of unoccupied stools at the far end of the bar. He took a seat on the middle one and held up one finger when the barman came his way.

"Gracias." He laid an American nickel on the bar and watched it disappear even more quickly than his beer had arrived.

Mexican beer had a fine reputation. After sampling one, Longarm concluded that the reputation was damn well earned. He couldn't have found anything better at home. He tasted the beer first, to test and enjoy the crisp flavor, then squeezed a wedge of lime the bartender provided and dropped it into the beer as well. The combination was excellent.

Funny thing, though. He already knew about lime in beer. And he liked it. But he wouldn't have considered putting lime or lemon juice in his beer back home in Denver. He might in El Paso, but never in Denver. That wasn't logical now that he reflected on it. Sure was true though.

Human nature. It can be quirky at times. Longarm shrugged.

He had another deep swallow and felt a very light and tentative touch on his elbow.

"Senor?"

To say that the girl was pretty was an understatement. She was stunning. He doubted she was more than seventeen if she was that old, and she had the taut, unblemished flesh of youth. She had a dark complexion, huge dark eyes, cheekbones that were sufficiently prominent to suggest some *Indio* in her blood and a waist that Longarm thought a man could probably put his hand around. One hand, that is. Using two would be cheating.

She stood, he guessed, five feet tall and wouldn't weigh as much as a good roping saddle.

Her hair was brushed to a high gloss and hung to her butt.

She was smiling at him. No real surprise there, of course. She really was about the prettiest little thing he'd seen in a long time, though.

Longarm laughed.

"Yes, *senor*? I am fonny to you?" She looked offended.

"No, hon. Not you. I was just thinking about something. Something I said to a friend o' mine this morning."

"Yes? And this makes you to laugh?"

"Yes, it does, honey. It surely does. But no offense t' you."

"Aw right then." She smiled at him again.

A pretty fifteen year old with hair down to her butt was what he'd told Carlton a little while ago. Well, this one probably wasn't fifteen. But she wasn't far over it. And she was damn sure pretty enough.

Longarm began to grin.

"Tell me something, honey."

"*Si, senor*?"

"How much would you charge for, say, a week's work?"

The girl's eyes went wide. "A week, *senor*?"

"Yep. Paid up front. You look like an honest girl."

"Aiii! One week. I would . . . five pesos, *senor*? It would not be too much?"

"Honey, I wouldn't low-grade you like that. How about ten? But I only have dollars. No pesos. Would ten dollars American be enough for a week?"

She looked like manna had just started falling from heaven. But then to her way of thinking maybe it had. "*Senor*, anything you want. Anything. You know? You jus' tell me, an' I will do."

She raised onto her tiptoes and tried to give him a kiss,

but she wasn't near tall enough, even when she put her arms around his neck and attempted to pull herself high enough to reach him.

Longarm laughed and wrapped his arm around her waist to lift her high enough so she could kiss his cheek. Lifting her wasn't much more difficult than picking up the tankard of beer had been.

"Would you like some lunch before we go over to the El Paso side, honey?"

"*Si,*" she said and added a burst of incomprehensible Spanish. He could tell by the excitement in her eyes, though, that whatever she said, she was mighty pleased by the transaction.

Anᕌ yeah, this one was most definitely a fine-looking filly and then some.

Sure did beat any of the virgin sisters that were being hawked by small boys all up and down the street, he thought.

Longarm left the rest of his beer sitting unheeded on the bar and walked out into the bright sunlight with a very happy little *senorita* clinging to his arm.

Chapter 11

It took him a few minutes to remember where the house was so he could tell the hack driver, but he got there eventually. The place he wanted was a tidy cottage that had an unkempt flower bed slowly dying in the front and an equally neglected vegetable garden in the back yard. A single cottonwood stood on the south side, offering shade from the heat of the sun.

The girl clucked unhappily at the sight of the shape the plantings were in. "Needs water," she said.

"You're right, honey." Longarm led the way up the steps onto the front porch. "Say, what is your name anyhow?"

"Anita."

"Pretty name," he said. "Pretty girl."

She smiled.

The front door was locked. Longarm reached up to feel his way along the top of the frame over the door and brought down a rusty, dust-covered skeleton key. He could have jimmied the lock as easily as looking for the key and probably done it quicker. But it was more polite to use the key, he figured.

He opened the door and held it for Anita to pass through ahead of him, then followed.

"Make yourself at home," he suggested, removing his Stetson and tossing it onto a table that sat beside the sofa.

He could smell something—soap, he thought. Fresh. He went to investigate.

Carlton had been home since this morning when Longarm saw him at the police station. He'd had time to change his clothes and shave. The basin and towel in the kitchen were still wet, as was the cake of shaving soap and the brush in the mug on a shelf beneath the mirror.

Longarm hoped Carlton was able to get a catnap too, because it was beginning to look like he would be on duty continuously through the night again until tomorrow morning. Perhaps then Worrell would feel up to coming back to work and Carlton could come home.

To his surprise.

Longarm only wished he could be there to see the expression on Carlton's face when he walked in and found Anita waiting for him.

He considered trying to arrange that. Take Carlton to breakfast and then drop him here at the house before going over to Del Norte to collect Jurneman. After all, it wasn't like there would be any point to getting across the river too early in the day.

Captain Fernandez did not strike Longarm as the most efficient bureaucrat in the neighborhood. But then this was a neighborhood that was notorious for its inefficiency. Probably the good captain fit right in.

Still, it wouldn't be a good idea for Longarm to be here when Carlton discovered he was no longer alone in the house. If Longarm were there Carlton wouldn't be able to rip his clothes off and jump into the middle of the pretty girl. And Carlton being able to get his ashes hauled for the first time since Doreen died was the reason Longarm was going to all this trouble. It would be good for him.

47

Almost like a first time. For the second time.

Longarm chuckled and went to see what had become of Anita.

She was in the bedroom, he discovered.

And she was naked.

Very naked. And very, *very* pretty.

It's a funny thing about that. A mature woman always looks her best when she is clothed. Hair properly done. Makeup, if any, applied with care. Jewelry selected and worn just so.

But a young girl like Anita—with flesh as smooth and golden as fresh cream, skin without wrinkle or blemish, tits as firm and perky as if sculpted from alabaster—Anita was even more stunning when she was naked than she'd been when he first laid eyes on her.

Her pubis was covered with a thatch of short, dark fur. Her tits were barely more than a mouthful, yet because of her impossibly tiny waist—with so little waist and belly it seemed incredible there would be room enough in there for her internal organs—those little boobies were perfect in shape and proportion.

She tossed her head, deliberately throwing sheets of black, silky hair out of the way so he could better see and admire her. Then, she bent slightly and shook her head again to bring the cascade of hair to the front and, straightening, turned around so he could see her from the back also.

There was no flesh to spare on her back, which was formed in a perfect V-shape—wide at the shoulders, narrowing across her shoulder blades, down a ladder of vertebrae and finally reaching that waist. Longarm had seen horse shoes with a circumference larger than Anita's belt would be.

And below that? Her ass was as round as an apple and as pretty as a sunrise. Cute. Definitely cute.

Anita gave him a moment to admire what she had to

offer. Then she made a quarter turn to her left, showing herself in profile as she peered at him over one canted shoulder, her left foot lifted at the heel so as to show off slim, incredibly lovely legs.

Longarm had a hard-on. He couldn't help it. He'd brought the girl here for Carlton, not himself.

But. . . .

"Senor?" Anita's smile was sweet. Charming. And she was so pretty.

She held her hand out to him.

He walked nearer. Reached up to cup his face gently between her hands, then let them slide down. Onto his chest. His stomach. She began to unfasten the buttons at his fly.

She could see the bulge in his britches. There was no way he could have hidden that throbbing flagpole.

Longarm opened his mouth. To explain. To apologize. To tell her that she was here to meet his friend's needs, not his own.

The only thing that escaped his lips was a groan because by that time Anita had his trousers unbuttoned and his cock free.

She dropped to her knees and lightly, tenderly kissed the tip of his pecker. Her breath was warm on his engorged flesh. And the sensation changed from warm to hot when she slowly sucked him into her mouth.

She tipped her head back a little and looked up at him with delighted, laughing eyes as she continued to suck while she cupped his balls in both hands and at the same time lightly tickled his asshole.

Longarm groaned again.

Later.

He could . . . speak with . . . Anita . . . about Carlton . . . later.

"Ahhhhh!"

Chapter 12

Longarm felt like he'd been wrung dry. Limp and empty. And almighty good. Lordy, but that little gal from across the border was a joy to romp with. Carlton was in for a treat.

Longarm finished explaining the real reason Anita was there. She did not seem to mind in the slightest that she was expected to service two different gentlemen during her term of employment. She was a sweet girl, willing to do whatever was asked of her and even come up with some ideas of her own while she was doing it.

So he dressed and let himself out after giving the girl final instructions on just how she should greet Carlton when he came home tomorrow morning. He figured if she met Carlton just exactly like she'd handled him a few hours earlier, everything would be just fine.

Carlton's house was close enough to the hotel that he did not bother looking for a hack. He didn't mind walking, and in fact rather enjoyed it. He lighted a cheroot and set off at a long-legged pace that covered ground with deceptive speed. A normal walk should cover roughly three miles in an hour's time. Longarm's gait carried him closer to four miles in that time without hurrying.

At that rate, the walk back to the hotel took him about twenty minutes. Not that it mattered. He hadn't anywhere he needed to be nor anything he had to do until tomorrow morning when he would go back across the border to collect Adolph Jurneman.

He reached the hotel and mounted the board sidewalk in front of it. He figured he would clean up just a little—certain parts of·his person were sticky with a mixture of juices and needed sponging off. Then he'd go have a bite to eat. Maybe drop by a saloon for a drink and perhaps a game of cards. Then. . . .

Aw, damn!

He snapped his fingers. He'd forgotten to arrange for Anita to have supper. And she would need breakfast too before Carlton got there and was able to attend to her further comfort.

Dammit anyhow.

Longarm had reached the front door of the hotel but stopped and spun on his heels so he could go back to Carlton's house and take care of Anita. He. . . .

Something slammed into the wooden siding on the hotel front wall beside his ear, a sound like that of a heavy hammer slamming onto hard oak.

A heartbeat later, the sound of that impact was followed by the dull bark of a gunshot.

Longarm dropped into a crouch and spun to face the threat. His Colt was in his hand already although he had no conscious recollection of drawing it.

Enough light remained from the late afternoon sun to show him a faint stream of white gunsmoke drifting away from the mouth of an alley across the street.

Longarm snapped a shot blindly into the alley, certain he would not hit anything but aware that not too many men will stand still when there are bullets coming toward them.

Another gunshot blasted out of the alley mouth, but this

time the shooter was standing too far back inside the protection of the alley for Longarm even to see the smoke from his shot. The bullet thumped loud but harmless into the back of a rocking chair a good twenty feet away from where Longarm stood. *Good!* The gunman, whoever he was, was spooked. The chair began to rock as if some unseen hand had tipped it back.

Longarm took the opportunity and charged straight at the alley mouth. Hopefully the SOB in there wouldn't be expecting that.

He caught a glimpse of movement at the corner of the haberdashery beside the alley and fired again.

A voice cried out, the sound loud and sharp after the booming reports of the pistol shots.

Longarm continued his straight-on charge, ignoring what was probably a ruse intended to make him drop his vigilance.

He ran hard across the street, then bent low as he leaped the last few paces. As he reached the alley and threw himself across the opening, he triggered two quick shots into a figure he glimpsed leaning against the haberdashery wall.

Longarm came up short against the wall on the other side of the alley, using it to stop his run. The muzzle of the Colt maintained its aim at the man who stood there.

There was no need for Longarm to shoot again, however.

The man—dark hair, medium height, stocky build, with a Remington .44-40 dangling from the fingers of his right hand, now held low at his side—wore a look of blank surprise.

He stared at Longarm, then down at his chest where blood was beginning to spread down his chest and belly, and seeping into the waistband of his black-and-gray striped trousers. He looked at Longarm again.

"You have killed me, I think."

"Why'd you shoot at me?" Longarm asked.

The man—Longarm could see now that he was Mexican, probably in his early- to mid-thirties—gave Longarm a wan smile.

His right hand twitched. It might've been an involuntary muscle contraction. Might just as easily have been an attempt by the ambusher to take this one last chance to put a bullet into an adversary.

Longarm didn't know the truth and never would. He was not a man who believed in taking unnecessary chances. He raised his Colt and put a finishing bullet into the fellow's forehead.

The man's head snapped back, rebounding off the haberdashery wall and leaving large amounts of blood and gray goo behind it. When his lifeless head fell forward again it took his body with it. The Mexican dropped face first into the dirt. His body fell with the same dull, hollow sound of a slab of meat being dropped onto a butcher's chopping block.

Longarm looked dispassionately down at the man he'd just killed.

He had no regrets. But he sure did have some questions he would've liked to ask this *hombre*.

With a shrug, Longarm first looked around to make sure no other threat seemed imminent, then reached into his coat pocket for cartridges. He began to reload the big Colt.

Chapter 13

"Hold it right there, mister."

The policeman looked like he was about fourteen years old. Or possibly it was just that Longarm was getting to an age when any young man looked like a runny-nosed kid. "Mind if I exhale?" Longarm asked, smoke from his cheroot wreathing his face as more than sound escaped from his mouth.

"I'm serious, mister. Don't move."

Longarm was hunkered down on the sidewalk, his back against the haberdashery wall and the cheroot trapped between his teeth. The reloaded Colt was in the holster where it belonged. But Longarm's right hand rested within inches of the butt and the young policeman was damn-all lucky that it was a fellow officer he was bracing like that and not some lunatic looking for an excuse to kill someone else.

The El Paso policeman's revolver was still in its holster, secured in place by a flap of leather and a metal snap. Instead of wielding a gun, he tried to intimidate his suspect with a wooden baton that he waved like he believed it was a magic wand. "On your feet, mister. Turn around. I'm going to have to handcuff you."

Longarm tried not to laugh. He did manage to hold it

down to a very small chuckle. "Son, calm down here." He rose to his full height, towering over the policeman when he did so. "My name is Custis Long. I'm a deputy United States marshal. And I shot this man in self-defense."

"You're Long? Marshal Mitchell said you were in town. I . . . I've heard about you, Marshal. They say. . . ." He did not finish telling Longarm what "they" were saying nowadays. Instead he peered down at the dead man, who was pale from loss of blood. The policeman turned even more pale, but then he had a head start, the dead man being Mexican.

"Ever have to kill anybody?" Longarm asked him.

The cop shook his head. "No, sir."

"If you're lucky, you never will."

"Yes, sir."

"But if you don't learn to have your gun in hand when you go to arrest someone, especially someone you think may have committed murder, you may find yourself on the wrong side of a homicide. Put the stick away when it comes to serious crime, son. Be prepared to defend yourself if you have to."

"Yes, sir."

"You can put the handcuffs away too now. Unless you still intend to use them."

The policeman looked down and seemed mildly startled to discover that he still had his handcuffs in hand. He shoved them back into a pouch on his belt and dropped the baton into a leather socket also on the belt. He was wearing a loose-fitting blue jacket with shiny brass buttons and a blue cap with a leather bill attached. Longarm's opinion was that the get-up made the young policeman look more like a railroad conductor than an officer of the law. But he was sure the city fathers had their reasons to require such an outfit. The reason, Longarm suspected, would probably have something to do with a uniform salesman in some politician's family.

"Sorry, sir."

"Can you take care of this body for me? I don't know how you like to handle such things here."

"Yes, sir, of course."

"Fine. And you can tell Carlton I'll drop by the station later to fill out a report?"

"Yes, sir."

"One other thing. Have whoever picks up the corpse take it by the station for Carlton to look at. Maybe he or somebody else there will recognize the guy. I went through the pockets but didn't find anything that would identify him, and I'd kind of like to know who he was. Kinda like to know why he shot at me too for that matter."

"Yes, sir. I'll do that."

"Is there anything else you need from me, son?"

"No, sir. Thank you, sir."

Longarm considered passing along some other lessons. One being that a police officer should take any claims of identity with a grain of salt. Longarm announced himself as a federal officer. But the kid hadn't asked for any proof of that. Longarm could as easily have been an escapee from a mental asylum as a deputy U.S. marshal for all the young cop knew.

Still, too many comments and corrections tend to cause resentment rather than learning. Longarm would be satisfied if the kid took heed of his warning about the gun versus that baton. That one could save his life someday.

"Tell Carlton I'll stand treat for supper when I come by to fill out that report for you."

"Yes, sir."

Longarm walked across the street to the hotel—no one shot at him this time—so he could quickly freshen up, then go back and take some food to the girl.

Now that there were things piling up that he needed to do, though, he thought he would hire a cab instead of doing any more hiking around El Paso.

Chapter 14

"I don't know his proper name," Carlton said, "but his nickname is the Matador. They say he was the best there was with a knife. Killed God knows how many men on both sides of the border. All that is pure rumor and reputation, though. None of the killings were proven. Far as I know, he hasn't ever been charged with any." Carlton dryly added, "Won't be now, of course. Looks like he was lucky. Got away with every one of his killings."

"Yeah. Right. Lucky indeed." Longarm reached for his coffee cup. "Well I wouldn't know how good this Matador was with a blade. But he wasn't so great with a pistol, I can tell you that for certain sure."

They were eating at a restaurant not far from the city hall police station. The people there obviously knew Carlton and brought him steak and eggs without being asked. Longarm ordered the same.

Mexican beefsteak, he figured. Not that it tasted any different. It was the cheap price that led to his assessment of the origin. For generations, rustlers crossed the border to steal cattle, take them back across and sell them cheap. The Texans did it. So did the Mexicans. And for that matter so did Arizonans, New Mexicans and—for all

Longarm knew—Californians, too. Border rustling had become a time-honored profession, prosecuted on neither side since no laws were broken in the jurisdiction where the rustlers lived and did the selling.

"Good beef," he said now with a silent compliment to whatever wealthy don unwittingly contributed such quality to the meal.

"They put out a good meal here." Carlton broke the yolk on one of his fried eggs and sopped it up with a piece of fluffy biscuit. "Any idea why the Matador wanted you dead?"

"Shit, I was hoping you could tell me," Longarm said. "First thing I knew was when that bullet hit the wall beside me. I hadn't seen him there an' never saw him any time before neither. Whatever the reason, I don't think it could have been anything personal."

"Robbery?" Carlton said, more as a question than a suggestion.

Longarm shook his head. "I don't think so. Not from way the hell across the street like that. If he was looking for a robbery victim, it would've been some poor sonuvabitch smaller and more prosperous looking than me. And it would've been close up so he could cut, grab an' run. You said he was known for his knife, not his gun."

"True enough." Carlton sawed off a bite of tender steak and speared it with his fork.

Carlton looked pretty good, Longarm thought. Tired as hell of course. His eyes were rimmed red from lack of sleep and he was in need of a shave. But apart from that, Longarm thought he looked better now than he had when he'd been fresh and rested. It was doing without the whiskey while he was on duty that was good for him, Longarm suspected. With any kind of luck, little Anita would revive Carlton's interest in living again and he'd quit drinking so heavily.

Not that Longarm had mentioned anything about the

pretty girl. He still intended that to come as a surprise. In the meantime, Anita seemed content with having enough food in the house now to feed her for days if need be.

"The only person I've had a cross word with since I got here is your Sergeant Worrell," Longarm said. "I have to admit that he's crossed my mind as a possibility. He could damn sure be mad enough—an' crazy enough—to want me dead. But would he be the sort to hire the job done instead of trying to ambush me his own self an' get that satisfaction, too?"

"Jeez, I hope not." Carlton pondered the question for a minute or so, chewing slowly with an absent expression while he considered it. Eventually he shook his head. "I don't think so."

"You don't sound real certain," Longarm said.

"I can't give you any guarantees," Carlton said, "but it doesn't seem like the sort of thing Ronny would try. Not using the Matador anyway. I know the assholes Ronny runs around with. Most of them are no better than he is. Birds of a feather flock together and all that. I think if Ronny did decide to get somebody else to take you—and I'm not saying it's impossible, considering that he'd have a perfect alibi from being laid up in bed right now—I really think he would get one of them to do the job. Not some Mexican who's known for belly-to-belly knife work." Carlton made a face. "Or more likely belly to back. I don't think he was the sort to go face-to-face unless he didn't have any choice about it.

"As for Ronny Worrell though, it just doesn't fit." Carlton shook his head again. "He'd more likely use one of his pals on this side of the border."

"All right. You know him better than I ever want to. I'll accept your judgment, Carlton. Won't completely forget about Worrell, but I'll move him to second place on my list of suspects."

"And the top spot would belong to . . . ?"

Longarm grinned. "Damn if I know. May never know, in fact, seeing as how I expect to have Jurneman in custody an' be on my way back t' Denver some time tomorrow."

"If you're willing to let it go like that."

Longarm shrugged. "The guy is dead. Could be I'll have to let it go."

"And in the meantime?"

"I don't claim I'll forget about it, exactly. I'm still interested. Did this Matador guy work for anybody in particular?"

Carlton shook his head. "Not that I know of. Lay enough gold on his palm and he was your boy. But I haven't heard much about him for the past six or seven months. You want me to ask around? Somebody on that side of the border might know something we don't."

"If it wouldn't be any bother for you, I'd appreciate it," Longarm told him.

"No bother. We swap information back and forth all the time. I can go across tomorrow morning after I get off duty."

"Huh uh. Not tomorrow. I don't need t' know that quick. An' you'll need some sleep. You're already dead on your feet. Tomorrow you go home straight-away an' go to bed. Comes to that, you can mail me whatever you learn. A fellow likes to know who wants his scalp, but I'm not so curious that I'd stay down here looking for personal revenge. Soon as I have my prisoner I'll leave."

"I'll go across tomorrow afternoon then, if I wake up in time."

"Fair enough," Longarm said, although with an unspoken reservation about that likelihood. Not after Anita got done wearing him out. Carlton would be lucky to wake up in time to go on duty, never mind getting up early enough to make a trip across to Del Norte beforehand.

"They have good desserts here, Longarm," his friend

suggested. "Miz Torres makes the best peach pie you've ever put in your mouth."

Longarm was tempted. He did dearly love a slab of good peach pie. But dammit he didn't want to become over-full.

He'd promised Anita—the girl had practically twisted his arm to make him do it—that he'd come by again this evening to keep her company. She said she'd be scared to stay all alone in a strange house that was not even in her own country. Real scared, she'd assured him.

Not that she looked particularly scared when she said it. But what did he know about a young girl's sensitivity?

She'd wheedled the promise out of him and now that it was made, well, he hadn't any choice in the matter. None at all.

So no, he concluded, it wouldn't do for him to be too full to properly enjoy whatever it was that Anita might have in mind for the evening's entertainment.

A little piece of that, he figured, would make for a better dessert than any kind of pie.

"Reckon I'll skip the pie this time," he told Carlton.

Chapter 15

Young flesh. It is smoother. Tighter. More elastic than a mature woman's skin.

It's no wonder, Longarm reflected, that once a woman gets into her thirties or thereabouts she will do almost anything in an effort—a hopeless effort at that—to try and regain the taut neck and belly of her youth. Pack themselves in smelly mud, bathe in goat's milk, smear themselves with honey and cream. It was silly, Longarm thought, but sad, too. He was sure that Gladys, bless her lusty-busty heart, would cheerfully take a bath in mule piss if somebody told her it would tighten her flesh and give her the skin of a sixteen year old again.

Longarm sighed and splayed his fingers wide across Anita's flat, taut belly. He'd pulled out of her and rolled off to the side not two minutes ago yet the feel of her flesh beneath his hand brought the tingling stir of renewed arousal back into his loins.

Not that he was complaining.

He turned his head and licked and nibbled at the small, rose colored button of nipple closest to him. Anita sighed and arched her back, lifting herself to him.

"You like that?"

"Si." She smiled. "I like." The smile turned to laughter, and she rolled onto her side facing him, taking the nipple away from him but offering herself for a long, deep kiss instead. Longarm figured the trade-off was all right by him.

Her lips were soft and mobile. Her tongue sweet and penetrating. She pressed herself tight against his body, and he could feel the heat of her. The sleeping soldier began to come alive again.

When Anita felt his stirring, she laughed once more and used the fingertips of one very small hand to press Longarm flat onto the bed in Carlton's spare room. Strong men could not take Longarm down; Anita accomplished it with ease.

"You are tired," she said. "Let me do this, yes?" she whispered.

"Yes," he agreed without bothering to ask for details.

Anita raised herself onto one elbow and poised above him. She looked deep into his eyes, gave a tender smile, then she dipped her head. Her hair hung loose in a cool, silky curtain that surrounded both their faces. She kissed him, taking her time about it, tasting him, promising unspoken things that would all be done for his pleasure alone.

"You are nice," she whispered.

"Thank you. *Gracias.*"

She kissed the point of his chin. His throat. His neck.

Her tongue explored the channels of his ear. Its tip slid gently, quivering inside the ear.

The tongue, warm and moist, licked and fluttered down the side of his neck. Onto his throat again. His collarbone.

She found his nipple and suckled there, the sensation surprisingly intense. Anita remained there for a while, licking and sucking, while her free hand played lightly over his stomach. Crept lower, her fingers twining into his public hair.

She found his erection, full and eager again, so quickly after the last time. She wrapped her fingers around the shaft and squeezed. Hard. Then again more gently. She whispered something that he could not hear; his own nipple in the girl's mouth muffled whatever it was that she said to him.

Anita took her time attending to that nipple, then moved to the other and gave it an almost equal amount of attention before the searching, probing, ever-eager tongue moved lower. Across his belly. Stopped for a while to investigate the depths of his navel. Found the base of his cock and licked its way upward to the tip.

"You like this," she said in a soft voice.

"I like this," Longarm agreed, his voice sounding more like a croak than a whisper.

Anita peeled the foreskin back from the tip of his cock and ran her tongue around and around the shiny, bulbous head.

Longarm heard a groan. It took him a moment to realize that he himself had made the sound.

That seemed to please the girl. She chuckled. The head of his dick happened to be inside her mouth at that moment, and the feeling caused by the tiny movements of her throat and tongue almost drove him past the point of control. He desperately wanted to thrust his hips upward and send his cock plunging into Anita's throat but he managed, barely, to restrain the desire.

Anita apparently felt or somehow sensed his desire, for she chuckled again, deliberately this time, and then raised up onto her knees so she could move close to Longarm's side—his cock still inside her pretty mouth—and poise there above him.

She hesitated for a moment, and he could feel her swallow. He got the impression she was preparing herself for something, although he did not know what that might be.

And then she showed him.

Anita opened her lips wide, took a deep breath—he could feel the cool air pass over his hot, wet dick—and then pressed herself onto Longarm's shaft.

Longarm could feel a momentary resistance when his prick passed through Anita's mouth and into the back of her throat.

She pressed herself onto him until the full length of his shaft was inside her and her chin was pressing forcefully into the pad of hair at the base of his cock.

Longarm cried out. The feeling . . . so tight . . . so hot . . . was fantastic.

He reached down and gently stroked the back of Anita's head, careful to not apply any pressure that might make her think he was demanding that she continue to hold him so very deep inside her mouth and throat. He had no idea if she could breath when she had him in there like that, and he did not want to hurt or frighten her.

After a moment she withdrew. But not all the way. She pulled back only far enough that he was in her mouth but not her throat.

And then she thrust down onto him again.

Longarm let go then and allowed the trembling in his hips and the hot, insistent sap in his balls to take over.

He cried out and spewed a stream of come so deep inside Anita that she probably never tasted it.

He came and then, fully satiated, he collapsed, limp and empty and completely contented.

Chapter 16

"Senor?"

"Fernandez. *Capitan* Ignacio Fernandez." This was the fourth or fifth time he'd said it. It was obvious the corporal spoke no English. But dammit, the man's name was the same in either language. "Captain Fernandez," Longarm said one last, hopelessly helpless time.

"You wish to see the captain," a voice came from behind him.

Longarm turned. The gentleman was tall and thin, built like a rapier. He was probably as handsome a man as Longarm ever saw and there was something about him that said he was strong, rich and intelligent. An hidalgo to be sure. "Yes, I would. I was supposed to meet him here this morning." Longarm introduced himself.

"I am Joaquin Figaroa, *Senor* Long."

"And you are . . . ?"

Figaroa spread his hands and smiled. "I am but a passerby," he said. Longarm did not believe that for a moment. This was a man who had influence. Whether he also had office or title was immaterial. "How may I help you, deputy?"

Longarm explained the nature of the problem. "All I

need is to collect Adolph Jurneman and be on my way. It's all been cleared through your ambassador in Washington, sir."

"Ah, I see." Figaroa's smile was dazzling. "This should be no problem, *senor*. You have the necessary papers?"

"Yes, of course. I gave them to Captain Fernandez yesterday."

Figaroa turned to the corporal and briefly questioned him, listened for a few moments and inquired again. Eventually he turned back to Longarm. His expression was grave. "I am so sorry, *senor*. Captain Fernandez has not yet reported to . . . excuse me . . . for, reported *for* duty."

"Does the corporal know where he is?" Longarm asked.

"Sadly, he does not," the tall gentleman responded.

"What about the papers I left with him?"

Figaroa exchanged more comments with the corporal, who then proceeded to search through the desk where Fernandez sat the day before. He found nothing.

Figaroa gave more instructions and the corporal disappeared into the depths of the building, only to return some minutes later with empty hands.

"I am truly sorry, *senor*. Capitan Fernandez must have the papers with him." Figaroa's expression became cheerful. "Perhaps the captain even now is attending to the release of your prisoner."

"Perhaps he is at that, sir," Longarm said politely. And tomorrow pigs may fly and cows shit silver pesos too, he silently mused.

"Is there a further assistance I may offer?" Figaroa asked.

"No, sir. You've been very kind."

"If you would care to wait . . . ?"

"That prisoner is the reason I've come all this way, *senor*. I expect I can sit and wait a spell."

"Very well, deputy." Figaroa turned and gave instructions to the corporal before informing Longarm, "There is a bench in the small room there. When Capitan Fernandez returns, you will be informed at once."

"Thank you, *senor*. You're a big help and I appreciate it. *Gracias, senor. Muy gracias.*"

Figaroa bowed—he was not wearing a sword, but Longarm thought he should be, if only for the sake of appearance—and said something more to the corporal before leaving the Del Norte city hall.

Longarm unhappily went in the direction the gentleman had indicated. The room was small and airless and the bench uncomfortable. But if Captain Fernandez had duties to perform, well, so did Longarm. He sat. And waited.

According to the Ingersol—he had to look at his watch to gauge the passage of time, because there was no window in the waiting room—it was nearly 3 P.M. and there was still no sign of Fernandez. And until the captain showed up, it was clear there would be no getting Jurneman. Dammit.

Longarm wandered out into the lobby. The corporal had been replaced at the desk by a young private. He didn't speak English either. This was becoming frustrating. "Fernandez? *Captain Fernandez?*" The repeated inquiries brought only shrugs and smiles in return. Eventually Longarm gave up.

His stomach was rumbling. He'd had a light breakfast and nothing since.

"If Captain Fernandez comes in . . . aw, forget it." The private's expression was benign but entirely uncomprehending. "I'll be back," Longarm said.

He turned and headed off in search of something to eat.

Chapter 17

"Hello, Longarm."

"Howdy, Carlton." His friend looked well-rested, wide awake and . . . relaxed. There was no sign of Anita, and Carlton didn't utter a word about the girl.

But Longarm noticed that Carlton did not invite him inside. He wondered just what state the girl was in since Carlton wouldn't welcome him in.

"It's a little late for me to go across the border with you now," Carlton said. "I have to be on duty in less than an hour."

"That's all right. I'm afraid I'll still be here t'morrow."

"No luck with getting your prisoner I take it."

Longarm shook his head. "Not hardly. I spent this whole damn day over there and never so much as got to talk to anybody about it. Fella I was waiting for, the one that promised he'd get it done for me, didn't bother t' come t' work today."

Mitchell reached inside the door to fetch his hat and gunbelt, then stepped out onto the porch without giving Longarm much of a chance to see past him into the house. Longarm thought that was kinda funny—humor funny, not odd—but of course did not come right out and say so.

"Who are you dealing with over there?" Carlton asked as he closed the door and led the way down the steps to the street.

"A captain named Ignacio Fernandez."

"Nacho?" Carlton laughed. "No wonder you haven't gotten anywhere yet. Good old Nacho. You can count on him. Count on him to promise the moon and stars. But he won't deliver as much as a clod of mud, Longarm, until you slip him a little something under the table. That's what's holding up your deal. Nacho won't give you squat until you give him a reason to. Anything in your budget for bribes?" Carlton chuckled a little more.

Longarm grunted. "I could put it down as . . . I dunno. Horse rental. Something on that order." He smiled. "I kinda doubt the Justice Department would approve *mordida* as a legitimate expense even if I could get my boss to go along with it. How big an expense d'you think I'm looking at here?"

"Oh, not a lot. In fact, I wouldn't want you to offer him very much. That would spoil it for the rest of us. Make the son of a bitch greedy. I'd say ten dollars would be generous."

"Hell, I can manage that."

"Tomorrow tell whoever is on the desk that you need to see the captain *muy pronto*. Give the desk man fifty cents and you can be sure the message will reach Nacho. And when you offer the bribe, for God's sake don't call it a bribe or you'll offend him. If you do that you're guaranteed to get nowhere. Tell him you realize there will be processing fees. And tell him you will pay the fees when you have the prisoner in your custody. Don't offer to pay up front. Delivery first, then payment. Otherwise he'll hit you up for more at the last minute."

"I'm not a virgin when it comes to bribery, Carlton.

70

An' I know how t' be discrete when I have to."

"Why, Custis! I'm surprised. I wouldn't have thought it of you."

"*Giving* bribes, Carlton. Giving them."

Mitchell snickered. "Sorry. Guess I misunderstood."

"Yeah. Right."

They reached the cafe that Carlton favored and went inside. The waitress on duty was a gap-toothed, big-eyed little girl of twelve or thirteen, almost certainly the owner's daughter. She was about as skinny as a corn shuck scarecrow, but as bright and bubbly as a fountain. "Hi, Uncle C. The usual for you? Is this your friend? My name is Ella. What's yours?" She paused, but only because she had to take a breath before she went to chattering again. Longarm liked her.

Eventually they were able to slide some answers in amid the flow of Ella's questions and comments. Breakfast for Carlton. More of that good Mexican beef and fried spuds for Longarm. Ella suspended her flow of chatter to spin away and run into the kitchen to place their order.

"Cute kid," Longarm observed.

"For a fact," Carlton agreed.

Ella came back with coffee and a plate of dinner rolls hot out of the oven. Longarm grabbed a roll and slathered it thick with butter. "Damn but it's nice to have some regular food. My stomach is kinda upset from the lunch I had over in Del Norte. Couldn't find anything but some greasy tortillas wrapped around a wad of cold refried beans."

"I know a place on that side where you can get some fine beefsteak. Tender and juicy and marbled with fat."

"American raised?"

"Of course."

Longarm sighed. Things were definitely different down here on the border. He was glad he worked out of Denver. "I wish everybody on that side could be as sharp as the fella I met over there this morning."

71

"Oh? Who's that?"

"Guy named Joaquin Figaroa. He helped me when I was trying to get the guy on the desk to find Fernandez for me. I liked Figaroa. He seemed—is something wrong? You're looking at me funny."

"Are you sure he said his name is Figaroa? *Joaquin* Figaroa?"

"That's what he told me," Longarm said around a mouthful of soft yeast roll. "How come that surprises you?"

"And he was at city hall?"

"Yeah, that's right."

Ella came back with their food. She saw they were busy talking and did not interrupt. But Longarm thought she did look a mite disappointed that she couldn't join in the adult conversation with them. She made a face and went scurrying back to the kitchen.

"You don't happen to know what he was doing there, do you? Or who he was seeing?"

"No, of course not. He came out—I don't know from where—while I was there near the entrance. Saw I was having trouble and offered to help. He translated for me. That's all. Why? What's so special about him?"

"For one thing, that beef on your plate probably belonged to Don Pedro Figaroa. Joaquin is the oldest son. The Figaroas own about half the state of Chihuahua, Longarm, and three fourths of the beef raised there."

"Thought he looked like a don," Longarm said.

"Oh, he's that all right. But Joaquin . . . I wonder what the hell he was doing in the city. He usually stays away. He has enemies. Political enemies. I hear that Joaquin has political ambition himself. They say he's aiming to be governor at the very least. Maybe president of the republic. Except if Joaquin and the Figaroas get into power, rumor has it there won't be a republic much longer. The family supported Maximillian a while back, and the way

72

I understand it they got the idea then that being emperor would beat hell out of being president. No annoyances like voting or opposition parties or dissent, if you see what I mean."

"I'll be damned. You sure about that, Carlton?"

"No, I'm not certain sure. But it's what I hear."

Longarm grunted. "Fortunately it isn't something I have t' worry about. Prob'ly you don't either. And I still say that I liked him. If they were all as sharp as him, things would go smoother over there."

"You going to have some of that pie today?" Carlton asked.

"If it's that good, I suppose I should. Just to check up on your judgment." Longarm motioned for Ella and placed an order for two slabs of her mother's peach pie.

Chapter 18

Longarm and Carlton Mitchell sauntered out of the cafe with their bellies full of good food and hot coffee.

"You were right," Longarm said. "The pie really is that good."

"What? You doubted me?"

Longarm grinned around the toothpick between his lips and said nothing. Carlton opened his mouth to speak, but before he could they heard Ella call out to them as she burst from the cafe doorway and came running after them. "Uncle C, Uncle C, wait! You forgot your box of matches."

The girl's feet pounded on the wooden sidewalk boards. Carlton turned to meet her, and Longarm stopped to wait for them. He reached inside his coat to fetch an after-dinner cheroot.

"Jesus!" Carlton blurted. "Get down, Ella, get down!"

Longarm spun around in response to the urgency in Carlton's voice. The girl was in the middle of the sidewalk and behind her at the corner of the building a man had stepped into view with a double-barreled scattergun in his hands.

Carlton grabbed Ella and lifted her bodily, twisting to the side and heaving her into the street.

74

Longarm went for his Colt but the man with the shotgun already had his weapon cocked and leveled.

Both muzzles blossomed with fire and white smoke,
and Longarm heard the quick, bee-buzz zip of heavy-
gauge shots whistling past.

Longarm's shot was not more than half a heartbeat behind that of the shotgunner. His .44-40 Colt spat lead and
flame, the first slug taking the gunman square on his
breastbone, the second striking with a dull slap into his
stomach and a third ripping out the side of his throat.

A fountain of bright blood arced high into the air where
it dissolved into a scatter of mist and tiny droplets. The
late afternoon sun streamed through the blood mist and
created a rainbow.

The gunman may have seen it. If so it was his final
sight on earth and the impression he would carry with
him into hell. He dropped to his knees and toppled face
forward onto the sidewalk, the empty shotgun falling from
the dead man's hands with a clatter.

"Uncle C! Dear God, wake up! Uncle C!"

Longarm shook himself as if coming out of a trance
and looked around. Ella was kneeling beside Carlton who
was also down, blood beginning to spread across his vest
and onto his trousers.

"Aw, dammit," Longarm blurted. He raised his revolver, an impulse filled with hate and anger, and aim it
toward the shotgunner.

But that SOB was already dead, and shooting him again
would accomplish nothing.

"Ella honey, run get a doctor." He dropped to his knees
beside his old friend. "I'll look after Uncle C till you get
back, honey."

The girl gave Longarm a stricken look, then jumped to
her feet and bolted away down the street as people began
to poke their noses out of windows and doorways so they
could see.

Chapter 19

He said he was a doctor and he had the obligatory black satchel and seemed to know what he was doing. But if Longarm only saw him on the street and was asked to guess at the man's occupation, he would have thought it something on the order of a mulewhacker or a lumberjack.

The doctor was a good two inches taller than Longarm and had the physique of a young ox. Or perhaps that of an oversized statue depicting Paul Bunyan. He had a ruddy complexion, piercing gray eyes and a blue-black beard that probably required shaving morning, noon and again in the evening to keep it under control.

His hands, however, were as gentle as they were large. He came at a run and dropped down beside Longarm and a supine Carlton Mitchell.

"You're doing fine, Marshal. Just fine," the doctor said in a soothing voice. He smiled reassuringly as he brought out scissors that he used to cut away Carlton's vest and shirt to expose the wounds.

At least five pellets from the would-be assassin's gun had struck Carlton. Two in the upper chest. One grazing his side. One inflicting a bloody but essentially harmless slice on the side of his neck. And then there was one that entered Carlton's body right off the center line of his torso, just beneath the rib cage. That small wound, not half the size of a dime, welled up and overflowed dark blood with each breath Carlton took.

And those breaths were becoming labored. The frothy bubbles that showed at the lower of the two chest wounds told Longarm that—at the very least—Carlton's lung was punctured.

The doctor used a wad of bandage lint saturated in grain alcohol to clean the wounds so he could assess them. Then, moving with a sure and deft speed, he brought a gum plaster from his bag and applied it over the lung wound to seal it off. Carlton's breathing eased almost immediately.

"Help me, mister. I need to get him back to my office for immediate surgery."

"Looks t' me like you have it under control," Longarm said with considerable relief.

The doctor gave him a hard look. "Don't count your chickens, mister. The lung wound is just an annoyance. It's this one here that worries me. If it entered the marshal's liver . . . well . . . it won't be good. I need to get him on the table and under ether right away so I can open his belly and see if I can repair whatever damage I find there. Now will you help me, please?"

Longarm and the doctor managed to pick Carlton up off the sidewalk and carry him down the street. Townspeople trailed behind like the wake left by a fast moving pirogue. Little Ella was among them, as was her mother.

"This way," the doctor said, pointing with his chin.

The office was upstairs. A sign painted onto the frosted door glass identified the doctor as J. M. Quayne, Surgeon and General Practitioner. Quayne kicked the door open impatiently and hurried inside, Longarm hustling to keep up.

"In here."

The surgery was in a small room at the front of the building. A padded table equipped with thick canvas strapping and heavy buckles dominated the room. On one wall were several small cabinets carrying ranks of wide, flat drawers not four inches thick.

"We'll put his head here. Help me now. Get those straps on him. Make sure you bind him tight. It's for his own good."

"You there."

Longarm hadn't realized Ella and her mother were still with them, but both now stood at the entrance to the surgery.

"You'll find reflector lamps mounted on metal stands. In the back room there. Get them for me. All of them. I need them trimmed and filled and lighted. Do that now, please."

Both Mrs. Torres and Ella hurried to do as the doctor said.

"That's good. Make sure his arms are pinned. No, don't worry about his head. I'll immobilize that with some clamps and a rest so he'll not be trying to carry the weight. You'll see. Right. Tighter on that forearm and wrist, if you please. We don't want him moving about and harming himself."

While Quayne was giving instructions to the others, Longarm was busy placing oddly-shaped steel instruments onto trays where the doctor could reach them, laying out lint and bandages, setting out bottles and a framework of thin metal that fitted over Carlton's nose and mouth. That frame would hold folds of muslin onto which ether could be dripped in just the correct quantities desired. Too much and the patient would die from the anesthetic; too little and the pain could drive him deeper into shock and he might die from that.

"You," Quayne said, looking at Longarm. "You'll drip the ether for me. Two drops every time I nod. No more.

No less. Now get over here beside his head where I need you." He raised his voice and bellowed, "Lamps. Where are my lamps?"

"Coming. Right away."

Quayne removed his coat and rolled up his sleeves. He had thick wrists and as much hair on his arms as a bear.

But he damn sure seemed to know what he was doing.

Longarm figured Carlton was in good hands here. Lordy, but he sure as hell hoped so.

Ella and her mother brought the lamps into the small room and positioned them as Quayne directed. Then he told them, "You'd best leave now. Wouldn't be good for you to watch this. The healing arts aren't gentle."

Little Ella already looked sickened by the sight of the ugly shotgun wounds on the man she called Uncle C.

"Go on now," Quayne said, his voice gentle but firm.

"Are you ready, sir?"

Longarm nodded.

"Two drops then. Count to five. Two more drops. Do that until I tell you."

"Right."

"And don't talk. Just do what I tell you. I don't need any distractions."

Longarm almost spoke in response. Then realized. He nodded instead and with a hand as steady as if he were squeezing a trigger, he began applying the ether under the doctor's direction.

Quayne picked up a scalpel, a long handle with a tiny, paddle-shaped and exceptionally sharp knife blade at the end of it.

The doctor paused for a moment, head tipped back and eyes closed. His lips fluttered slightly. He was praying, Longarm thought. Which probably was a pretty good idea.

With a wad of lint in one hand to help stanch the bleeding and the scalpel poised in the other, Dr. Quayne touched the sharp blade to flesh and made his first cut.

Chapter 20

Longarm wiped his forehead and took out a cheroot. It had been hot during surgery under the glare of the reflector lamps, and the heat—or something—was very tiring. He snapped a match aflame and lighted the cigar, then pulled out the Ingersol. It had been—he hadn't realized it was anything like that long—more than three and a half hours.

It was pitch dark outside now and was close to ten o'clock at night.

"What d'you think, doc?" he asked.

"I think I need a drink," Quayne said. "And a cigar. I don't suppose you'd have one of those to spare."

Longarm gave him a cheroot and lighted it. "Can't help you with the drink though."

"That's all right. I have something right here." Quayne opened a filing cabinet and brought out a bottle of brandy. "Join me?"

"No, thanks."

The doctor shrugged and helped himself to one small swallow taken direct from the bottle. No need for a glass. He carefully replaced the cork and returned the bottle to the cabinet.

"Be damned if you look like a doctor," Longarm said. He meant that when it came to appearance, but over the past few hours he'd learned that Quayne was not only a doctor, he was a good one too.

Quayne grinned. "I decided early on that I wanted to study at a proper college of medicine and not apprentice myself to some quack whose abilities I wouldn't have knowledge enough to judge for myself. Paid my way through school by prizefighting. Two bouts every Friday night, one on Saturdays. Lick my wounds on Sundays and back to the books on Mondays." He laughed and touched the bridge of his nose. "I was a pretty good-looking guy until then. By the time I graduated, my face started to resemble a turnip. Which is why you see me as I am today, a humbled but happy man."

"Good at what you do, too." Longarm extended a hand and introduced himself. It was something they hadn't gotten around to before.

"Call me Jim, Longarm."

Longarm nodded. "Tell me the truth, Jim. What are Carlton's chances?"

Quayne opened his mouth to speak, then hesitated. "I wouldn't say this to his family, but you being a U.S. marshal . . . There *is* a possibility he could recover, Longarm. It's a slim chance, but I suppose that's better than nothing. I did what I could in there. Now it's out of my hands."

"You'll keep an eye on him?"

"Of course, and I have some ladies who are good about sitting up with a patient and taking care of things when I'm sleeping or tending to someone else. Soon as I finish this cigar and have a moment to send for them, your friend will not spend another moment alone—until we know. One way or the other."

"Good enough. Thank you."

Quayne walked to the office door and tried to open it. The knob rattled but the door did not open. "Huh. I guess

Miz Torres set the lock when she and Ella left." He smiled. "I'd pretty much forgotten this door has a lock. Longarm."

"Yes?"

"There's a note pinned to the door here."

"Yes?"

"They want you to come to the police station immediately."

That made sense, Longarm thought. There would be witnesses to the shooting of course, but the best information would come from a participant. Besides, Carlton's colleagues were bound to be worried about him. "I'll go right away then, Jim. And thank you. From both of us."

Quayne nodded, unlocked the door, and said, "If you see a youngster who'd like to earn a nickel, send him up here, would you? I need to call my nurses in and I don't want to leave the patient while I do that."

"I'll make sure of it," Longarm promised and let himself out, leaving the door open to provide a little fresh air inside the hot, stuffy office where Carlton lay fighting for his life.

"You're Long, aren't you?"

"That's right," Longarm admitted to the young officer who was on duty at the police desk.

"The deputy chief wanted to see you first when you showed up."

"Fine by me."

The officer pointed down a short corridor and said, "His name is Deputy Chief Fielder."

Longarm smiled. "Never met a man before with the first name of Deputy."

"It's really Norman. But you know what I mean."

"Sure." Longarm started off in the direction the cop indicated.

"Marshal."

"Yes?"

"How is Constable Mitchell?"

"Too soon t' tell," Longarm said.

Constable? he asked himself as he ambled down the hall. What would they think of next?

"I want you to know that I've sent a telegraphic message to your employer asking that you be recalled and someone else sent down here to replace you," the deputy chief of police said by way of greeting.

Norman Fielder was in his late 30s or early 40s and looked like a man on his way up the political ladder. He wore a handsomely tailored suit, a pencil-thin mustache and had hair slicked down so hard and glossy it looked like it was a painted-on and polished fake. Apparently he was above any necessity to bother with things like guns and badges and all that. It seemed fairly obvious that this was an administrator, not a lawman.

"Nice t' meet you too," Longarm responded, slouching into a chair in front of Fielder's desk and crossing his legs. He'd finished a smoke only minutes earlier but took out another one and gave it his full attention as he trimmed and lighted it. With any luck Deputy Chief Fielder would be allergic to cigar smoke. It was obvious that Fielder was predisposed to dislike Longarm and that was just as well, because Longarm would damn sure hate it if he disliked the son of a bitch and found that Fielder liked him anyway. That sort of thing could be awkward, but this way—both of them ready to snap assholes at first sight—worked out nice and tidy.

"You've been causing trouble for this department ever since you showed up, Long. First, you maim my best sergeant. Now, my night constable has been shot down and is dying."

"You don't know that Carlton is dying, dammit," Longarm snapped.

Fielder ignored the interruption. "I probably should charge you with manslaughter for that fiasco out in the street this evening."

"Fine by me. Be all right if I charge you with obstruction of a federal officer in the performance of his duties?"

"Fuck you, Long. I know all about you. I'm not impressed."

"I don't know jack shit about you, Fielder, and I'm not impressed either. Does that make us a pair?"

"If Mitchell dies, it will be your fault."

"I notice you haven't asked how the surgery went," Longarm said.

"Anything I want to know, I will get from sources I trust. For now, what I want is for you to take the next coach out of my city."

"This is a free country, Fielder. A man is allowed to wish for anything he damn pleases." Longarm smiled around the thin barrel of his cheroot and added, "Doesn't mean he'll get what he wants. But he's free t' want it."

"I mean it, Long. I want you out of this city."

"An' I intend t' leave, Fielder. Quick as I'm done here, me and my prisoner will be headed north. By the way. Who was the man I shot out there this afternoon? And have you looked into whether your man Worrell is behind the murder attempts?"

"Get out of my sight, Long. And get out of my city. I want you on the first stage north. Or else."

" 'Or else?' Or else *what*, you deskbound asshole?" Longarm stood and leaned over Fielder's desk until he was eyeball to eyeball with the man. A plume of smoke lifted off the cheroot that was still clamped between Longarm's teeth. Longarm positioned himself so the smoke curled into Fielder's eyes, forcing the man to pull back from the confrontation.

"Well?" Longarm demanded.

When Fielder had nothing else to add to his empty

threat, Longarm straightened to his full height so that he towered over the seated administrator, glared at the man for half a moment more and then stalked out of the deputy chief's office.

Chapter 21

Anita uttered a piercingly loud cry of anguish and damn near collapsed when Longarm showed up at Carlton's door and explained the situation to her. Longarm did not know what in hell to do with the shrieking, sobbing, distraught young girl. He settled for grabbing and hugging her in the hope she would soon calm down. She did not.

Eventually, though, the sobs became muted and less frequent. The thing that truly amazed Longarm was that this outpouring from Anita seemed genuine.

The girl was a whore, for crying out loud. A cheap bordertown whore. And she'd been with Carlton . . . what? . . . one day?

Yet Longarm was convinced that Anita's concern was sincere. She seemed honestly to care about Carlton and his survival. Unlike Fielder, who hadn't even bothered to accept information about the man when Longarm offered it.

Sometimes, Longarm reflected, you just never know.

The wailing subsided and was replaced by a low, agonized keening sound from the girl, but in time even that dissipated and she was still. By then the front of Longarm's shirt was soaked with tears and snot. At least not very much of the mess reached his vest, which was harder to clean and for which he had no replacement in his bag.

The girl said something to him in Spanish, then backed up and tried again in English. "You take me to heem, yes?"

Longarm did not hesitate. Doctor Jim said he needed help watching over the patient. Why not Anita? "Sure. Come with me."

Anita wiped her eyes and straightened her dress and followed Longarm out into the night.

Dr. Quayne was delighted to have the help. His regulars were already busy, he said, one with the preparations for a funeral and the others with one thing or another. "I was afraid I was going to have to do this all by myself."

Anita first gave Carlton a complete looking over that included very carefully lifting the edge of his bandage so she could personally inspect Quayne's needlework. Then she wiped Carlton's forehead, gave him a tender kiss and began bustling around the room rearranging things to her liking.

She was, it seemed, in charge here now.

Longarm looked at the doctor and shrugged. He got a grin back in return. The two men tiptoed out of the recovery room, leaving Carlton in what seemed to be very good hands indeed

"I'm sorry, sir. We're under orders to not tell you nothing," the young desk officer said. "The chief an' the deputy chief, too. They've told us clear, we aren't to say nothing to you."

It was morning and a different officer was pulling desk duty, but the story was the same now as it had been the night before. Deputy U.S. Marshal Custis Long was persona non grata insofar as the El Paso Police Department was concerned.

"I see. Well, thank you for being honest about it, son."

"It isn't . . . it ain't up to us, Marshal. I'm real sorry."

"I understand." He turned to leave.

"Marshal."

"Yes?"

"Constable Mitchell. How is he this mornin'?"

Longarm smiled. "Holding his own the last I saw," he reported. That was true as far as it went. He hoped it remained so after the long night.

The young man smiled. "I'll spread the word to the rest of the boys. An . . . I guess I shouldn't ought to say this, neither, but . . . I'm glad you got the son of a bitch that shot him, Marshal. Thanks."

Longarm nodded and made his way out onto the street again. It was obvious he would not accomplish anything at the police station.

It occurred to him that this young man and presumably the others as well were assuming that Carlton was the target of that backshooter yesterday evening. Assuming that the man with the scattergun hit the person he intended. Longarm rather doubted that. It would be one hell of a longshot coincidence for someone who wanted Carlton Mitchell dead to make the attempt while he just happened to be walking beside Custis Long, who was also was the recent object of an attempted assassination.

No sir, that would be a mighty long coincidence. And Longarm had no faith whatsoever in the likelihood of coincidence in such matters.

Longarm himself was the target, he suspected, and Carlton took the buckshot simply because the little girl got in the way. Carlton saved her bacon and Longarm's at the same time.

But Lordy Lordy, Longarm thought, he hoped Carlton hadn't done that at the expense of his own life. He did not deserve that in exchange for such a selfless act.

He went from city hall to Dr. Quayne's office and let himself in without knocking. There was no sign of the doctor, but when Longarm peeped inside the surgery where Carlton still lay, Anita was still there. When Longarm looked in, she was busy dipping a cloth into cooling water, wringing it nearly dry and then using it to bathe Carlton's haggard, bewhiskered face.

Carlton's complexion looked like wax, Longarm thought. Yellow and mottled and unhealthy. Longarm had seen that before, usually not very long before someone gave up the ghost and slipped away into death.

When she saw Longarm standing there, the girl gave him an expression that was probably intended to be a smile. Instead it looked more like a grim declaration of war. She was not going to allow Carlton to die. She simply wasn't.

Longarm touched the brim of his Stetson to her in a silent salute and slipped back outside again. He'd learned what he wanted to know: Carlton was still alive. And as long as life remained, there was yet hope.

From the doctor's office Longarm walked the short distance to the Torres's cafe. There was no evidence now of the gunplay and death that occurred there less than eighteen hours earlier.

"Mornin'," he said when he walked in and removed his hat.

Mrs. Torres came running to him and a moment later her husband rushed out from the kitchen as well. The daughter was not present. Probably in school, Longarm thought, despite her recent bout of terror.

The thanks Longarm received were overwhelming to the point of embarrassment. "I'm not the one you need t' be thanking," Longarm said. "Save that for Carlton."

"We have been to mass already this morning, *senor*. We have lighted candles in his name and offered our prayers," Torres said.

Longarm nodded. "I reckon that's what he needs

more'n anything right now. I shoulda thought of it myself."

"Please, *senor*. You are hungry? You will do us the
honor to eat with us?"

He hadn't gotten around to having any breakfast yet
and now at the mention of food his mouth watered and
his belly rumbled. "I would, thank you. I'd also like t'
ask you some questions if you don't mind. The police
don't want t' talk to me, and I'm hoping maybe you can
help out a little."

"Anything, *senor*. We are in your debt for the life of
our baby. Anything we have is yours."

"Just a little information. That's what will help me the
most."

Torres and his wife conferred back and forth for a minute in Spanish, then Mrs. Torres took off for the kitchen
while Torres led Longarm to a table where they could sit
and talk.

Chapter 22

"His name," Torres said, "was Jonathon Marcus. Not a good man."

"No," Longarm agreed, "I reckon not."

Torres shook his head. He was a thick-bodied man, beginning to gray at the temples. "This Marcus, he was a man of the alleys. You know what I mean, *senor?* Like a . . . " he paused to search for the word he wanted, ". . . a vermin. Hide in the shadows. Empty the pocket of someone who drink too much. Steal something here. Sell it there. Steal it back and sell it again. You know this kind of man, I think."

"Yes, I surely do. I take it you knew him then?"

"Oh yes. Here in this small place, many people come to eat. We hear things. We don't tell them so much. But we hear. We know."

Longarm nodded. "Did Marcus work for anybody in particular?"

"No, *senor*. No one in El Paso, no one in Del Norte would trust him to hire. Pay him for an unpleasantness perhaps. Like to shoot *Senor* Mitchell from behind. Marcus, he would do a thing like that for money."

"Big money?"

"Not so big, I think," Torres said. "A man of small importance, a man of small payment. He had gold in his pocket when he die. Fifty dollars in gold. A little more of silver."

"Fifty in hand. I reckon that would be part of what he was promised to do the shooting. An' prob'ly another payment when the job was done. A hundred dollars total for the murder, I'd judge."

Torres shrugged. "This I would not know."

"No, sir, an' I'm just guessing. D'you happen to know if Marcus was a friend of police Sergeant Ronny Worrell? You do know Worrell, do you?"

"Oh yes. I know this man too." He sniffed. "Not much better a man than Marcus. But I have never seen these two together. I have not heard of them being *compadres*."

"Marcus run with anybody in particular then?"

The cafe owner shrugged again. "He has friends. Evil like him. Mexican, *gringo*, the bad ones find each other and group together. Marcus, mostly he stay on the Del Norte side since, oh, three, four month ago. He had some trouble in El Paso."

"With the police?" Longarm was still thinking there might be a connection between Marcus and Worrell if only he could find it.

"No, *senor*. The police they are no problem. A pay-off here, a bluff there, a few days in the jail. Not so much big trouble from the police. Small things only. Marcus had trouble with the *Senor Kaufman*. I do not know what this trouble was, only that Marcus was frighten after it. I do not think he has been on this side of the river again since that time."

"I don't know Kaufman," Longarm said.

"*Senor* Kaufman, he is *El Jefe* in El Paso. The thieves, the *putas*, the street corner cheats and monte players, they all pay *Senor* Kaufman. Not so much. A little only. Like a tax, you would say. They pay or they have the broken arm, the broken leg."

"A protection racket," Longarm said. "Do you merchants have to pay him too?"

"Oh no, *senor*. The *Senor* Kaufman taxes only the ones who do not like the police, only those who cannot complain in the court."

"Did Marcus do any work for Kaufman before they had that falling out?"

Torres spread his hands. "I do not know this to be certain true, senor. But yes. Sometime for the *Senor* Kaufman, sometime for the *Senor* Guzman who is in Del Norte what the *Senor* Kaufman is in El Paso. The boss. You know?"

"So either one of those gents could have hired Marcus."

"It is possible, yes."

"Is shooting somebody the sort of thing Marcus would generally be expected to do?"

"No, *senor*. To pick the pocket of one already passed out, that would be a thing to expect of him. To come very quiet behind a man and bash him on the head, that one would expect of Marcus. But to shoot? No. I do not think he had a gun."

"How about a knife artist called the Matador? D'you know anything about him?"

"A little, *senor*. His proper name is Antonio Hernandez but he fancied himself a matador. They say he tried to earn the suit of lights but he lacked the *cojones* to stand before the bull, although I do not know this. It is only what is said. He is dead now, you know."

"Yes. I killed him."

"Ah."

"He tried to shoot me. Not his usual style, I'm told."

"No, *senor*. The Matador was one to use the knife, not the gun."

"This is two men getting into shooting scrapes lately

93

an' neither one of them known for that sort of work."

"This is passing strange, is it not?" Torres said.

"Yes, it certainly is."

Mrs. Torres came out of the kitchen bearing a tray that was almost too heavily loaded for her to manage. She'd piled it high with what looked like generous helpings of everything they owned back in the kitchen, starting with steak and running right through to flapjacks and three kinds of pie.

"Eat, *senor*. Eat."

Longarm figured this was how kings and princes and potentates ate. The Torreses had to pull a second table near in order to have enough room to spread it all out.

"Tell me, *senor*," he said before digging into the feast. "Where could I find this Kaufman fellow? I think I might have t' have a word with him."

Chapter 23

Longarm was full as a tick in a kennel of fox hounds when he walked out of the Torres's cafe. He wasn't as happy as he might have been though. They wouldn't let him pay a cent for all that food. It was embarrassing, but he hadn't wanted to push them too far about it. This was a way they could express their gratitude, and it would have hurt their feelings if he were to refuse them.

He checked his watch and hesitated. All declarations about taking the first possible stage aside, he wasn't going to leave El Paso before he got to the bottom of this shooting business. Shooting at him was one thing. He'd been shot at before. But wounding—and probably killing—a friend of his . . . that was something else again.

In the meantime, however, he had a job to do and he intended to get that done, too. He needed to get Adolph Jurneman in custody on the American side of the border. Any personal vendetta he might have against whoever was behind the Marcus and Hernandez assassination attempts took second place. First he would get Jurneman behind bars here in El Paso. Then he would do whatever it took to make sure Carlton Mitchell didn't die without somebody paying the price.

With a sigh he turned away from the El Paso business district and headed for the bridge across the Rio Grande.

"I am sorry, *senor. Capitan* Fernandez was here until no more than a quarter hour ago. He was expecting you, *senor*. He left instruction. When you come in you are to know that he is working very hard to accomplish what you require. That is what he does even at this moment." The Del Norte police lieutenant smiled. He was a handsome young man, resplendent in his uniform. "He says you should know that he expects to have the papers complete soon. You will return tomorrow, please. In the morning, yes?" The smile returned so bright and sincere that Longarm almost believed what the young man was saying. Almost.

Dammit, though, Longarm couldn't even offer the son of a bitch a bribe until he was face-to-face with him. Trying to negotiate something through a go-between like this younger officer would just complicate the situation and make it necessary to bribe more than just Ignacio Fernandez. Start that game and he could end up distributing money with a pitchfork to every man in uniform over here.

"Please give the captain my thanks an' tell him I'll be here tomorrow. A little earlier than today."

"*Gracias, senor*. Be assured the *capitan* will receive your message."

Longarm touched the brim of his hat and left. There wasn't any other choice about it.

Jim Quayne met Longarm at the door to his medical office. He laid a finger to his lips in a request for silence and motioned for Longarm to follow.

Anita lay asleep on a pallet of folded blankets. Carlton remained on the operating table, waxy and still.

"He looks . . . ," Longarm whispered, ". . . is he gone?"

Quayne shook his head. "That girl, she's amazing. She hadn't had a moment's sleep since she got here. I had to practically threaten her to get her to lie down a little while ago. Promised I'd keep an eye on him while she got some rest."

As quiet as the whispers were, Anita heard. Her eyes sprang open and she sat upright. Without taking the time to give Longarm a greeting, she rose to her knees so she was at eye level with Carlton. She felt his forehead and checked his breathing before she gently kissed him. Only then did she stand and turn her head to nod a hello.

Longarm entered the surgery and went around to the other side of the table. Carlton looked worse close up than he had from the door. And Anita looked almost as bad as her patient. She looked purely worn-out from her vigil.

Carlton's eyes fluttered. Opened. He looked left and right, saw Anita and smiled. She clutched his hand and kissed his fingers, each one in turn, then bent and kissed his lips. She whispered something that Longarm could not hear.

"Longarm." Carlton's voice was so faint Longarm at first wasn't sure he was hearing it.

"Hello, old friend."

"You got him?"

"I got him."

"Good. Anita."

"Si, mi corazon?"

"I have to . . . say something . . . to Longarm. You go get . . . something . . . to eat." Carlton's voice was no stronger than a newborn kitten's mewling.

"I am not hungry," Anita protested.

"All right but . . . go outside . . . just a minute."

The girl looked unhappy about the request, but she squeezed Carlton's hand and kissed him again and then very reluctantly left the surgery.

"Custis."

97

"Yes, Carlton?"

"Get Jim . . . in here . . . too."

Longarm motioned for Quayne to come near.

"You two . . . witness for me. Deathbed . . . will and testament."

"Carlton, you aren't gonna. . . ."

"Hush. Just listen."

"All right. Sorry."

"When I'm gone . . . the house . . . bank account . . . everything . . . goes . . . to the girl. You hear? All of it. You hear?"

"We hear," the doctor told him.

"Custis?"

"I hear, Carlton. But I reckon it'll be a long time before she inherits. You're gonna make it."

"She says . . . same thing." The old man managed a smile again. "Good reason . . . to get better. You know?"

"Yeah. I do know," Longarm told him.

"Just don't . . . tell her. Want to . . . surprise her. Okay?"

"Not a word," Quayne promised.

"Not one," Longarm said.

"Now you two . . . get the hell . . . outa here. Send . . . her in."

Anita came back into the room with a rush. She took Carlton's hand and held it to her cheek. Kissed him. Dipped a cloth into a basin of water and bathed his face and neck and hands again.

"If good care will pull him through, then he will make it," the doctor whispered when they were out of the earshot.

Longarm grinned. "Me, I'm counting on plain old horniness to provide enough reason for him t' live."

Quayne laughed. "If that's what works for him, I'll accept it."

"Is there anything I can do, Jim?" Longarm asked. "For any of the three of you?"

"Pray," the doctor said. "That's about all we have left to give him."

Longarm nodded. He thought about the Torreses who already had that part covered. And Anita who surely was adding prayers of her own. "I'll be back to check on him again from time to time."

"We'll be here. All three of us."

"I'm counting on it." Longarm went downstairs to street level and looked around, trying to orient himself in relation to the cafe and the directions Torres had given him to find *Senor* Kaufman.

He paused to light a cheroot and, without conscious thought, checked to make sure the Colt rested free and unencumbered in its holster before he started down the street.

Chapter 24

The law offices of T. Wade Kaufman and Associates occupied the entire second floor of the Kaufman Building.
And the Kaufman Building occupied half of an entire city
block. T. Wade Kaufman, it seemed, was a man of parts.
A man of the law, too. Or so it said on the sign. Longarm
always believed whatever a gold-lettered sign told him.
You bet he did.

The ground floor had a number of offices and small
shops laid out around a central lobby, from which a wide,
curving staircase ascended to Kaufman's private floor. T.
Wade Kaufman had himself a jim-dandy of a building
here, Longarm conceded. Marble floor. Gaslight chande-
liers. Hushed atmosphere. Oh, it was fine. Longarm stuck
the stub of his cheroot between his teeth and climbed the
stairs.

T. Wade Kaufman had a lobby of his very own on that
floor. Three men and one woman were in the waiting
room, which had a huge Persian carpet on the floor and
some obviously old and expensive paintings on the walls.
A reception desk was presided over by a woman whose
prim hair-do and high-collar dress failed to hide the fact
that she was a knock-out with generous lips and tits that

would have done a Brown Swiss milk cow proud.

Her smile of welcome was as dazzling as it was phony. "How may I help you, sir?"

The smile remained fixed so solidly in place that Longarm couldn't help wonder if it would slip any if he reached over and gave one of those knockers a hearty squeeze. "I need t' see Mr. Kaufman," he said, keeping his hands to himself.

"Of course, sir." She fetched a leather bound notebook from a desk drawer and opened it. "And what time is your appointment?"

Longarm dragged out his wallet and showed her the badge he carried there. "Mayhap this will do for an appointment."

The girl's smile never faltered. "Of course, sir. Wait right there, please."

Longarm sat. So did the girl. She bent her head and went back to doing whatever it was that she did at that desk other than smile pretty. Longarm sat there for about a minute, then stood and went back to stand before her again.

The smile returned in full force. "Yes, sir?"

"I'd like t' see Mr. Kaufman. Now."

"Yes, sir. I am sure he can fit you in very soon."

"Now," Longarm repeated in his most gentle, patient and understanding tone of voice.

"I am sure, sir, one of the attorneys will be able to accommodate you soon. Now if you will just wait right there—sir! Where do you think you are going, sir?"

There were two corridors extending sidewards from the central reception area. Longarm chose one and ambled into it.

"Sir!"

He ignored her and wandered on, reading the plaques screwed to the polished mahogany doors. Very nice woodwork in the place, he noticed.

101

"Sir!"

The girl's voice became more faint and soon was replaced by a man's voice. "Sir!"

Longarm turned. The man was young, handsome, with slicked-back hair and a mighty nicely tailored suit. He looked like he wouldn't know what to do with spit if he had a mouth full of it. "Are you Mr. Kaufman?"

"No, sir, but I am certain I can help you. Miss Everly tells me you are a policeman and you . . ."

"Miss Everly is wrong."

"But . . ."

"I'm a federal officer. Deputy United States marshal. I want t' see T. Wade Kaufman. I don't want t' dick around with receptionists or junior lawyers. Now do us both a favor an' point me toward Kaufman's office."

"I cannot do that, sir. Please state your business here, and I shall be glad to help you."

Longarm sighed. "All right. Fine. I really wanted t' do this the easy way, but if you won't have it then you won't, an' that's fine, too. So. Just t' make everything nice an' official, son . . . by the way, what's your name?"

"My name is Dillard Joyce, sir, and I am one of Mr. Kaufman's associates. As I said before, I will be glad to. . . ."

"You make sure pieces o' human shit don't have t' spend time in jail, do you? Never mind. Like I say, we'll do this right." Longarm brought the wallet out again and flipped it open. "Look it over close if you like."

"I accept that you are a deputy marshal, sir. Now if you would. . . ."

"Dillard, shut the fuck up."

The young man looked startled. Hell, maybe he'd never heard that word used before now, Longarm considered. Sure looked as if he hadn't.

"Thank you," Longarm told him. "Now let me make this nice an' simple so even a lawyer can follow it without confusing himself. Are you listenin' close, Dillard? Are you with me, boy?"

"I really think. . . ."

"Dillard, I won't tell you this again. Shut your fucking mouth. I'll let you know when you c'n talk."

Young Mr. Joyce looked ready to explode. He did so, however, without speaking again.

"Here's the deal, Dillard. You got two choices. You c'n show me—polite an' prompt—to Kaufman's door. Or you c'n be placed under arrest on a charge of interfering with an officer in the performance o' his duties. If you do that, Dillard, I am sure a smart lawyer fella like you can file motions for release under bond. But first I'll drag your young ass up t' Denver where you'll make a court appearance before the fed'ral judge presiding over this case. You with me, Dillard? Good. You'll remain in custody until you make that appearance before Judge Tomlinson in Denver. Right? Now. What'll it be, Dillard? Do I see Kaufman now? Or would you like t' get a taste o' what it is you been keeping your clients from?"

"I really do not see. . . ."

Longarm shrugged. And pulled out his handcuffs.

Chapter 25

T. Wade Kaufman was a fat man with a moon face, wire-rim Ben Franklin half-glasses and a fringe of graying hair that formed a puffy white halo that started above his ears and looped around the back of his head.

There was, however, nothing about him that was remotely angelic, nor was he in any way, shape or form the jolly fellow that fat men are supposed to be.

Wade Kaufman had eyes as friendly as the muzzles of a .44 and an expression that probably would break rock if he bore down and really tried. Judging from the look Kaufman gave Dillard Joyce when he ushered Longarm into the great man's office, Longarm felt sorry for the young lawyer the next time the boss got to him in private.

They'd walked in on a private conference between Kaufman and a client. The client, who was not introduced, looked like the sort of fellow one would expect to find lurking in a dark alley. Or, of course, in a lawyer's office. But then in Longarm's view the one place was about as murky and unpleasant as the other.

Dillard Joyce was busy stammering out apologies and explanations that no one was listening to when Longarm strode over to stand in front of the big, ugly son of a bitch in the client's chair. Without a word he pointed a finger at the man's forehead, then rolled his hand to the side and aimed his thumb toward the doorway.

The client seemed to have no trouble at all identifying Longarm as a lawman—the real thing, not a lawyer—and didn't quibble. He jumped to his feet and beat it for a clean getaway lest he might say or do something that would end up with steel clamped extra hard on his wrists. Longarm suspected if that were to happen it would not be a new experience for the man.

Kaufman's eyes narrowed, taking them down to a threat approximating that of a .32-20 instead of a .44. Longarm did not consider the change to be an improvement. "Who," he asked, "are you?"

Longarm told him.

Kaufman grunted. "I've heard of you. Nothing good, of course."

"T' tell you the truth, I feel better knowin' that." Longarm grinned. "Seein' as it comes from you."

"You don't know me."

"No, an' if you an' me cooperate just a little, I won't have any need to."

"Is that a threat, Long?"

"No, Mr. Kaufman, I don't threaten anyone. I do sometimes lay out alternatives. Like I did with your boy Joyce. Don't be too hard on the lad. I wasn't in any mood t' take no for an answer."

"Would you mind telling me what this is all about?" Kaufman asked.

"I expect you know Carlton Mitchell was shot down by a backshooter name of Jonathon Marcus."

"So I heard."

"An' what I heard was that Marcus owed you some favors."

"Do not draw unsubstantiated conclusions, Deputy. Jonathon Marcus was a former client of mine. He was not a business associate and he most certainly was not a friend."

"Word on the street is that Marcus coulda been trying to get back into your good graces by doing you a favor."

"The word on the street, Deputy, will also tell you that the moon is made of green cheese. Neither of those speculations is true."

"Then why would Jonathon Marcus be back on this side o' the border trying to gun somebody in the back?" Longarm asked.

"That question has a simple enough answer. Money. Marcus was a man of small means but large tastes. He would do anything for money. And being an exceptionally stupid man, he did not even have sense enough to charge a sensible price for his . . . shall we say . . . talents. Marcus came cheap. I am sure the price he requested in exchange for your murder would insult you."

Longarm raised an eyebrow. "Now that's interesting, Kaufman. You assume I was the target. It was Carlton that got shot."

"Now you insult me, sir. Of course you were Marcus's target just as you were the target of that preening idiot who styled himself *El Matador*."

"You know about that too."

"There is very little that happens in this town that I do not eventually hear, Deputy."

"An' neither one of them was workin' for you at the time," Longarm said. He reached into his coat, his eyes fixed carefully on the fat lawyer. Kaufman did not flinch.

Longarm brought out two cheroots and offered one to Kaufman. "No, thank you." He patted his chest. "Emphysema. I've had to give it up."

"Sorry t' hear that." Longarm returned one of the cigars to his pocket, then asked, "Bother you if I light up?"

"Please do. I still find the scent most enjoyable. But thank you for asking."

Longarm trimmed and carefully lighted his smoke. "You didn't say anything when I mentioned the possibility that those men might've had your interests in mind."

"What would you like me to say? That I did not do it? Of course I did not hire them. But then I would say the same thing whether I did or did not," Kaufman said. "As it happens, however, I did not. The proof of that is that in two separate attempts, neither of those incompetents succeeded. Had I wanted you dead, Deputy, I can assure you, you would now be dead. We are speaking hypothetically, of course."

"Of course," Longarm agreed, puffing a little white smoke toward Kaufman so the fat man could enjoy it too.

"Whoever hired those men is almost as great a fool as they were. One should not casually risk the ire of the law. As a lawyer, I know that better than most. The stakes would have to be very high indeed in order to induce an intelligent man to undertake so risky a venture. And frankly, Deputy, among the many things I have heard about you, none of them has been close to that kind of reputation. You do not accept bribes. I know of no double-crosses attributed to you that could lead to attempts at retribution. And the blunt fact is that anyone on this side of the border who has cause to fear you can escape your jurisdiction with no more effort than a five minute stroll across the bridge into Del Norte. Paying someone to kill you in El Paso would be, as the saying goes, overkill."

Longarm had his own opinion about what would happen if T. Wade Kaufman tried to hire him dead. But he did not bother going into it here and now. "You make a persuasive case, Kaufman."

"I deal in simple truth, Deputy." At least the man had the good grace to laugh at his own joke there. And so, in fact, did Longarm. He sort of liked a fellow, even a slime like lawyer Kaufman, who could laugh at himself.

"I'll think over what you've said," Longarm told him, rising to his feet.

"May I call you Longarm?" Kaufman asked.

"Yes." For a crime boss, Kaufman wasn't as bad as some might've been.

"Your inquiry here raises more questions than I can answer, Longarm, and a man in my position—" He grinned. "Never mind exactly what that position is but a man in my position likes to know why things happen as well as what happens. Information can be so useful, don't you know?" He spread his hands and smiled.

Longarm was finding this SOB more likable than he would have thought possible.

"I intend to make a few inquiries. On this side of the border and in Del Norte. If I find anything that I would care to pass along, I shall let you know."

"And in exchange?" Longarm asked. There would, quite naturally, be a quid pro quo involved, and he wanted to know what it was up front.

"Favors owed are like cash in the bank, Longarm." The fat man winked. "One of the secrets to my success."

"Fair enough," Longarm said, "but nothing that would compromise my limits."

"Understood," Kaufman agreed.

"In that case . . ." Longarm leaned forward and shook hands with the man. He hadn't intended to do that, but it seemed all right to him now. Surprisingly so.

"And Longarm," Kaufman said, as Longarm reached for the doorknob.

"Yes?"

"I hope Mitchell recovers." Kaufman smiled. "Even though he doesn't take bribes any more than you do."

The information was not surprising. Nor was the implied other side of that coin, which suggested there were police in El Paso who would turn a blind eye in exchange for personal gain.

Longarm let himself out of the handsomely-appointed private office and gave the buxom receptionist a cheerful salute on his way out.

Chapter 26

Dammit to hell anyway. The fool behind all this almost *had* to be Ronny Worrell. He hadn't had any difficulty with anybody else since he came to El Paso. Well, except for Marcus and *El Matador*, and they didn't count as they sure hadn't hired each other for a killing. And Longarm never saw nor heard of either one of them right up to the moment when they tried to kill him.

No, damn it, it had to be Worrell.

Longarm didn't much favor sneaking around. Not, at least, when a direct approach was available. He figured he'd just go have a talk with Sergeant Ronald Worrell, face-to-face and man-to-man. So from Kaufman's office he headed back to the police station.

There was a different officer behind the desk, a middle aged man with graying hair and a whiskey drinker's red-veined nose. "Sergeant Worrell on duty today?" Longarm was quite frankly hoping that this cop would not know who he was. Instead the man scowled and fixed Longarm with a most unwelcoming stare.

"You got no authority here, federal boy, so get your ass outa this station and outa this town."

Longarm smiled at him. "That's what I like to see.

Friendliness and cooperation between agencies. Has it occurred to you that I might be looking for the people who are responsible for Carlton Mitchell being shot?"

"Fuck you and him right along with you. I don't care who you're looking for or what you want. Get outa my sight or I'll lock you up for the night."

"You might have an interesting time doing that," Longarm said, his voice and expression mild. His eyes, however, glinted like polished steel and a surge of tension swept through him, bunching the muscles in his shoulders and tightening the flesh across the nape of his neck. "Are you gonna give it a try, buster?"

The desk man glared at him. But briefly. After a few moments, the officer's eyes drifted away from Longarm's challenging gaze. "Not right now."

"Yeah, well, you let me know if you change your mind. In front or from the back, whichever is your style."

The desk officer's jaw muscles bulged as he gritted his teeth and struggled to control his hate. "Damn you," he hissed.

Longarm touched the brim of his Stetson as if giving his good-bye to a woman, then turned and strolled out of city hall.

Apparently he would have to look elsewhere if he wanted to find out where he could find Worrell.

The bartender had a shot of rye whiskey waiting by the time Longarm crossed the room to reach the bar.

"Thanks." He dug into his pocket, found a silver peso— the exact equivalent to a dollar in its silver content and accepted as readily here as a U.S. coin would be—and laid it down. "I'm trying to find my friend Sergeant Worrell. Do you happen to know if he's returned to duty yet?"

The bartender laughed. "Not hardly. The way I hear it he's out on sick leave. Paid leave at that. They say it could

110

take him two, three weeks to recover from that beating he received in the line of duty."

"Hurt in the line of duty, was he?" Longarm mused.

"Oh yes. A bunch of street toughs jumped him while his back was turned. He was making an arrest at the time."

Longarm laughed. "A whole bunch of 'em, eh?"

"That's what I heard."

Longarm sipped the whiskey, sluicing it around in his mouth to gain the full flavor before he allowed it to trickle down his throat. It really wasn't bad stuff. "Your name is George, isn't it?"

"That's right."

Longarm introduced himself. George grinned. "I already knew that. It seems you've made an impression on this old town. Not all of it bad."

"Not all of it good either."

George just shrugged and smiled.

"Any idea where I can find my old friend Worrell?"

George pulled a turnip-shaped watch from under his apron and glanced at it. "It's just past noon. I'd guess Ronny would be at home still. Ought to be waking up along about now."

"You wouldn't happen t' know where he lives, would you?" Longarm asked.

"Sure. It's not but a block and a half." he gave directions to the place, then accepted Longarm's dollar and reached into the cash box for change.

"Keep it," Longarm said. He knocked back the remaining half shot of rye and thanked George for his help.

"Any time." George dropped the dollar into his apron pocket and rummaged in there for fifteen cents that he put into the cash box. Obviously George was an employee here and not the owner.

Ronny Worrell's house had seen better days. The front porch sagged, and one step was missing entirely. Longarm doubted the place had been painted since the day it was new, and the harsh El Paso sun had bleached and warped the clapboard siding. It would have been a as nice house had anyone bothered to keep it in a decent state of repair.

Not that that was any of Longarm's business.

He mounted the steps with care and chose his path across the front porch with equal caution lest he break one of the rotting boards and drop a foot through.

"Si, senor?" The woman who answered his knock was Mexican, with enormous breasts and a wild bird's nest of hair that looked like it hadn't been brushed since Methuselah was a young'n. She'd probably been a knockout twenty years ago. Now she looked like she had been knocked out. Even had the purple mouse under one eye to fortify that impression.

She was dressed in a cheap cotton wrap and was barefoot. She looked like she'd just gotten out of bed.

Longarm removed his Stetson and held it in both hands. "Sorry t' disturb you, ma'am. I'd like t' speak with Ronny."

"He's asleep."

"I'll bet he heard my knock too and woke up."

"He don't like visitors."

"That's okay, I don't like visiting." Longarm was smiling brightly, looking for all the world like a pleasant and helpful sort as he pulled the door further open and sidestepped the woman as he made his way uninvited into the interior of the house.

It took Longarm a moment for his eyes to adjust to the darkness. Outside the sun was almost viciously bright. Here the windows were heavily draped. That kept the light out. It also kept any air from circulating inside. The place smelled of old sweat and cheap whiskey and urine. Apparently no more maintenance was done inside the house than out.

Longarm did not have to ask directions to Worrell's

bedroom. From the left rear of the place he heard a querulous voice. "Bettina! Who was that? C'mere, you bitch, or I'll give you some more fist to eat. C'mere right now. You're gonna eat my cock or my fist, one or th' other."

When Longarm walked in, Worrell was sprawled on the filthy sheets of a brass bed. He was naked and had a hard-on standing at rigid attention. When he saw who the visitor was his expression fell. So did the hard-on.

"What does a man do with one that little?" Longarm asked pleasantly, his mocking gaze locked onto Worrell's sagging pecker. "Catch bugs an' fuck them, do you?" The truth was that Worrell looked to be of normal enough size. But what the hell.

"Get out of here. You got no right." Worrell reached under his pillow.

Longarm crossed the room in two strides and was there before Worrell could extract the Webley revolver from hiding. Longarm took hold of the pistol and twisted. Worrell tried to resist but his strength was no match for Longarm's. The gun came free. Longarm tripped the latch on the upper frame and opened the action. He turned the Webley over and allowed the six cartridges to fall clattering onto the bare floorboards. With a swipe of his boot Longarm kicked them underneath the bed.

He took hold of the pillowcase and yanked the pillow out from under Worrell's head. "No more surprises? Good." He dropped the now-empty Webley onto the bed and tossed the pillow down on top of it, covering half Worrell's bright red face when he did so.

Worrell sat up on the edge of the bed, and Longarm judiciously moved just far enough to the side to make sure Worrell did not return the same sort of kick that Longarm had given him lately.

"Get out of my house," Worrell snarled.

"Or what? You'll call a cop?"

"Get out."

"First we talk," Longarm said.

"I got nothing to say to you."

"All right. I'll talk and you'll listen. How's that sound?"

"Go fuck yourself."

"I'll take that to mean you're pledging your full co-operation."

Worrell gave Longarm what was probably supposed to be a withering look. It didn't work. Longarm failed to wither.

"Since you and I had our little . . . discussion . . . the one that gave you two weeks off with pay for your bravery in fighting off a whole gang of brigands . . . or so they seem t' think over at police headquarters . . . there've been two attempts made on my life."

"Yeah, I heard that. Damn shame they missed is all I can say."

"Well they did. And the only person in El Paso that I've had words with, the only one I can think of who might want to see me killed . . . ," Longarm reached down and grasped Worrell by the throat, yanking him off the bed to a standing position with Longarm's nose only inches from his. Ronny Worrell had a bad case of morning breath.

"What I'm thinking," Longarm said, "is that if anybody fucks with me again, I'll shoot them just like I did those first two and then I'll come back here, Ronny boy, and I'll put a slug in your· belly too. Low so it'll take you days, maybe even weeks before you die. You know what I mean, Ronny boy? In the gut. Right about here." Longarm's left hand completed the demonstration with a blow that would have doubled the sergeant over if he hadn't already been dangling from Longarm's right hand.

"Jesus!" Worrell gasped. "Don't . . . it wasn't me. I never. I don't even . . . I mean, sure, I know those guys. But I didn't hire them. I don't have any money for that

114

sort of shit. Ask anybody. I spend . . . I spend pretty good. You know? I never have the kind of money it'd take to hire a shooter."

"These boys both worked cheap, Ronny. And you could've promised them a free ride the next time they got in trouble with the law here. It wouldn't take cash with assholes like those two."

"I never, Long. Jesus God, I swear I never."

"You're my best suspect, Ronny, and my only one. That puts you square in my gun sights."

"No. Please."

Longarm gave a shove that sent the pale and trembling cop backward onto the bed, a trickle of piss dribbling out of his now almost invisible cock. There was no bluster in Sergeant Worrell now. Pathetic son of a bitch, Longarm thought.

Longarm turned to leave. Worrell's woman Bettina was standing silently in the doorway. The front of her kimono had fallen open, exposing dark bruises that covered her belly, hips and chest. It appeared that lover-boy Ronny liked to beat up on women in addition to his other more charming qualities. Longarm was rather glad now that Ronny would have a matching bruise to admire on his own pale belly. Bastard.

When Longarm brushed past her on his way out of the bedroom, Bettina did not respond even with her eyes. He might not have been there for all she seemed to care.

Chapter 27

Anita was still at Carlton's side, patiently sponging his forehead and temples with cool water. Longarm wasn't sure if Carlton was sleeping or comatose or simply resting.

"*Senor?*"

"Just checking on him," Longarm said. "I don't need anything. Don't want to wake him."

The girl nodded and went back to her self-appointed task.

There was no sign of Jim Quayne. Fernandez would not be back until tomorrow—if then—and Longarm had accomplished not a damn thing by talking with Kaufman and Worrell. He could have gotten discouraged if he really wanted to.

Instead he went downstairs to the street and went in search of a restaurant. It wasn't that he disliked the Torres's nearby cafe. Far from it. But he did not want to burden them with feeding him for the remainder of his stay in El Paso. Their gratitude was obvious and he'd enjoyed that one free meal. He did not, however, intend to let that become a habit.

There was a decent-looking place three blocks down

that was run by a buxom woman with graying hair, a complexion permanently made ruddy by the heat of a lifetime spent in kitchens and a personality that made strangers feel welcome.

"What will you have, friend?"

Longarm chose a table in a far corner where he would have the security of walls surrounding him—hard to be shot in the back that way—and contemplated what to order. It was late for lunch and early for supper, but he was hungry. And in no hurry. "Fetch out your biggest steak, ma'am. An' whatever fixings that come to hand."

She smiled and brought him a cup of coffee without being asked, then went off to fill his order.

Longarm stood and wandered through the otherwise-empty restaurant, peering at the seats of recently-vacated chairs until he found what he was looking for. A copy of the latest newspaper. He had patience enough when need be, but sitting idle while waiting for beef to burn was galling.

A small box on the front page told him about a special sale on spring buggies. Only $119, including a leather top. Heck of a deal he was sure, but he thought he'd let the opportunity go by.

A story in the news columns told about a change of command in the army's Department of Texas. Another mentioned rebellion fomenting anew south of the border— nothing unusual about that. And yet another informed him that the city's electrification project was lagging behind schedule, but the appropriate authorities were sure they would soon overcome all difficulties and complete the distribution of electricity to the city's merchants on time.

Longarm read each item with care and was making his way through the third-page advertisements when the smiling lady returned with his supper.

Smiling? She should have been laughing.

His own damn fault, of course.

He'd gone and asked for the biggest steak in the place. Well, she'd cooked it for him. She served it on a platter not a plate and even then it hung over the rim on the narrower edges. A mountain of mashed potatoes and a lake of creamed corn had to be served on a separate plate as there was no room for them on the meat platter.

This was the biggest dang steak Longarm ever saw, bar none.

It was also, he soon discovered, one of the toughest he'd ever encountered. Damn thing was half sinew and the other half gristle.

Longarm went at it gamely, but after a few minutes he was pretty sure the steak was winning.

The woman let him stew a while—and chew a while— before she came over to ask if everything was all right.

"Yes, ma'am. Nice flavor." Which was true, actually. The meat was tough but the taste wasn't bad.

She began to laugh and reached down to take the platter away. "Mister, I'm sorry, but I've been funning you. And believe me, you don't want to know where this beef came from."

"An old bull, I'd say," he guessed. "Maybe out of the bullfighting ring?"

"Something like that," she agreed. "Don't worry though. I just wanted to see what you'd say, and you're a plenty good sport. I have a good piece of meat for you in the kitchen. I'll be right back with it."

Longarm chuckled. "I did ask for the biggest you had, didn't I? Well, ma'am, I expect you brought it."

The replacement wasn't so large as the first steak had been, but this one was as tender as the first had been tough. He finished his meal with considerable pleasure.

Chapter 28

Longarm got a good night's sleep—a little too good actually; he wouldn't have minded a little company—and in the morning almost got into an argument with Torres over the question of whether Longarm should be allowed to pay for his breakfast. They agreed that he would. But Longarm had the impression that Mrs. Torres was reserving the right to slip in a few extras now and then.

From the Torres's conveniently located cafe he walked over to Jim Quayne's office. Carlton was asleep, but Longarm thought his color was improved. Anita was convinced he was mending.

At this point, Longarm thought the girl looked worse off than Carlton did. She was obviously exhausted, with under-eye bags as dark as soot marring her youthful beauty. It was just as obvious that she was determined to stay at Carlton's side no matter what.

"She amazes me, Longarm," Quayne said, not bothering to lower his voice. It was clear he did not mind if Anita overheard. "Do you know what she's been doing? She lifts the bandages and goes inside the wound itself. Wraps little balls of cotton tight onto the end of a long stick and dips that in carbolic, then goes inside the wound to clean and swab and tidy up in there.

"I never heard of such a thing. But I'll be damned if it doesn't seem to be working. I asked her about it. She never heard of that before either. But she tells me clean is good, and so she wants the old man's guts to be clean. She said she thought of it when she saw what the wound looked like after my surgery And the crazy thing is that it seems to be working. I expected to see signs of sepsis by now. Or smell it. But there isn't a peep nor a whiff of the rot you usually see in wounds like this.

"If I didn't know better as a doctor I'd almost start to believe along with her that he will live through this," Quayne said.

"My money is on the girl, Jim."

"By God I'm this close to joining you." Quayne added, demonstrating with his thumb and forefinger. "If this works I intend to write a paper on it for publication in the medical journals. See if we can't save a few lives with the method." He smiled. "I think I'll name the procedure for her, if so."

Longarm offered to pay for the doctor's services to date, but Quayne waved the suggestion away. "Nonsense. Besides, if this little girl's idea is successful, it will make me famous."

"All right, but let me know if you change your mind." Longarm shook the doctor's hand and went outside to find a cab that would take him across the border for another attempt at taking Adolph Jurneman into U.S. custody.

"What a shame, *senor*. The *capitan* was in his office early today. Already he has left. But he asks me to tell you that he is working dil . . . dil—he is doing very hard to have done the things of which you need."

Longarm scowled. But there wasn't a damn thing he could do, short of taking the young officer by the throat.

And he didn't think that would actually accomplish very much or he just might have given it a try. "All right, son, thank you. Any idea when I might be able to pick up my prisoner?"

"This afternoon, *senor*. Perhaps then." He smiled. "Or *mañana*."

"Yeah. Right." With a sigh of resignation, Longarm turned away from the desk and left the by-now all-too-familiar Del Norte city hall.

The cab he'd ridden across from El Paso was no longer there, so he lighted a cheroot and lengthened his stride as he headed back toward the border.

The Del Norte streets were pleasant, alive with pedestrians and vendors, chickens and dogs, dust and bright sunshine reflecting off the adobe walls. Longarm was enjoying the morning and the sights and sounds of the people around him.

And then there was . . . silence.

All of a sudden, the street he was on became silent, save for the low chuckle of a hen in search of a nesting spot. And the people were . . . missing. Gone. Scattered into doorways and alley mouths as if . . .

Longarm took a quick step to the side, into the lee of a column that stood at the entrance to someone's house. Something, by damn, was up, and the locals saw it coming even if he did not. He spun to look behind him, the big .44 in his hand without conscious thought as he searched for . . .

There!

Two men.

They looked ordinary enough in narrow-brimmed hats and ill-fitting suit coats. Like street vendors or workmen in search of a job.

Except these two were still on the street.

And these two carried straw mats rolled into stubby cylinders and laid over their arms.

As soon as they saw Longarm turn and look the two dropped their pretense and reached inside the mats. Each man brought out a sawed-off shotgun.

They were workmen, all right. But they already had been given work to do. Bloody work and the blood was supposed to be his.

The one on Longarm's left grabbed for the hammers of his scattergun. He had time to drag them back to full cock before Longarm could take careful aim and put a bullet into the man's chest.

The first one crumpled, his knees buckling and dropping him face forward onto the street.

The other swung the barrels of his shotgun toward Longarm and fired quickly from the hip.

The range was far for a shotgun, and there are damn few pellets in a charge of buckshot. Longarm heard the lead balls whistle past like a briskly moving swarm of bumblebees. One of them raised a puff of plaster dust from the column where Longarm stood. The others sailed harmlessly down the sidewalk. For a moment their multiple impacts sounded almost like rain.

Longarm manually cocked his double-action Colt so as to get a steadier hold and lighter trigger pull, then aimed deliberately low.

His slug slammed solidly into the meat of the Mexican's left thigh and the man staggered. Longarm shot him again, this time in the other leg, and the shooter fell. He was still alive though and still armed. Longarm wanted him alive. Did not particularly want him to remain armed.

"Drop the gun," he shouted.

He kept an eye on the two Mexicans, one of whom was still very much capable of returning fire while the other appeared to be dead. That of course might or might not have been the case. Playing possum is a time-honored ploy, regardless of nation or language.

"Drop your gun."

Eyes still fixed on the scene in the street half a block away, he moved swiftly by feel to eject the spent cartridges from his .44 and reload. He did not want to approach these two with a half empty revolver in hand.

Then, and only then, did he abandon the cover of the pale adobe column and venture out to see just what sort of game he'd bagged.

Chapter 29

Longarm felt like he was overseeing an armory. The
ground at his feet was awash in firearms. The two shotguns. Three large revolvers. One derringer. Two very
small hideout revolvers. Two stilettos. And one folding
knife with a very dull blade that would be useful for
cleaning a horse's hoof but not much more.

All of these came from the two Mexicans, the one dead
one and the other whose bitterly—and continuously—
voiced imprecations Longarm could not understand and
did not want to.

The good news was that he had this son of a bitch in
custody and still breathing. And that meant he was perfectly capable of answering questions. Starting with the
big one having to do with who hired him.

Or, Longarm was considering as an alternate possibility, who it was that directed them here. It was beginning
to seem less likely they were hired since neither man had
much money on him. Between them they couldn't buy a
big meal, so either they spent their advance money already
or their reasons for the shooting were not financial.

Well, well, well, Longarm thought with some wonder
as he watched the Mexican constabulary arrive, at least a

full squad of soldiers being led by a familiar gentleman.

The wounded Mexican, who'd been non-stop mouthy until the soldiers got there, clamped his jaw tight and settled for glaring daggers instead. Longarm considered that to be something of an improvement.

"Captain Fernandez," he said, "good morning. If I'd known this would bring you out of the woodwork, Captain, I would've shot a few of your citizens before this."

"Do not jest, *senor*. This is a most serious matter."

"Yes, it is, an' I'm getting kinda tired of it. Forgive me if I'm a mite testy. Bein' shot at sometimes does that to me."

Fernandez frowned but said nothing. He barked out some orders to his men, who had surrounded the shooting scene already.

A man wearing sergeant's stripes motioned toward the dead man and the prisoner, and two soldiers verified that the dead man was about as dead as he was likely to get, then turned their attention to the live one. They said something to him. The wounded man's response was delivered in a voice that was thick with loathing and, Longarm thought, with contempt as well.

"What's that?" Longarm asked.

"It does not concern you, *senor*," Fernandez said.

"The hell it doesn't. These two jaspers tried to shoot me in the back with shotguns. Anything this one says concerns the hell outa me."

Fernandez turned his back and barked at the soldiers, two of whom grabbed the wounded man by the arms and started dragging him away. The sergeant spoke and two others stepped forward to take the dead one by the ankles and drag him off also, his head bouncing along on the gravel of the dirt street.

The dead man couldn't feel that, of course. But Longarm couldn't help but wince anyway. It looked painful as shit.

"Where are you taking them?" Longarm asked. "I'll need to interrogate that guy with the shot-up legs."

"I will do that which is necessary," Fernandez said. "You have no authority here. I will let you know what I learn when I speak with this man."

Longarm had a whole hell of a lot confidence in that promise. Sure he did. "Captain, I'm the one they tried to kill. I need t' know what's going on here."

"And so I shall tell you as quickly as I know," Fernandez said grimly.

"While you're here, Captain, what's the deal with Adolph Jurneman? I need t' get him across the border and back to Colorado for trial. The paperwork is all in order, was before I ever got here, but you've been dragging your feet about turning the prisoner over to me like your government and mine already agreed. Why don't we go back so I can collect him and take him across now? Then you can do whatever you want with that prisoner and the dead sonuvabitch."

It seemed a good enough swap to Longarm. Fernandez didn't want to be pushed about these gunmen? Fine. Longarm would be glad to accommodate him on that subject. But he wanted Jurneman in return.

Fernandez gave Longarm the same sort of look he might have addressed to a cockroach crawling out of his tortilla, then turned and, without another word, strode purposefully off in the same direction the soldiers went with the wounded man and the dead shooter.

The sergeant formed up the remaining men and marched them away behind the captain.

The jumbled pile of weaponry remained behind on the street along with some dust-covered and coagulating rivulets of blood.

The weapons did not stay there long. As soon as the soldiers were ten or fifteen yards distant, a flock of street

126

urchins descended on the guns and knives. They disappeared in an eyeblink. The weapons and the children too, gone as suddenly and as completely as a wisp of smoke caught by a gust of hot wind.

Longarm idly wondered whether the street kids would use the weapons to rob somebody or settle for selling this unexpected manna from . . . well, not from heaven. Free enterprise at work either way, he figured.

Before the rest of the crowd dissipated, Longarm loudly asked, "Does anybody here speak English?"

A bent and aging man stepped forward. "I do, *senor*."

"Did you overhear everything that was said here, sir?"

"Yes, *senor*, for a truth I did."

"Then I'd like you to do some translating for me, sir. I'll pay for your time, of course."

The old man bowed. "It will be my pleasure to be of service, *senor*."

"Let's walk down t' that cafe I see on the corner. We'll have some coffee an' something to eat an' you can tell me just what it is that this,"—he pointed toward the bloody spot where the two shooters had leaked onto the street—"what this here was all about."

"As you wish, *senor*." The old man bowed again.

Longarm walked very slowly down the street, holding his pace down and his impatience under tight rein so the old Mexican could keep up.

Chapter 30

Longarm sat over a beer—very good, locally-brewed beer, in fact—while he pondered what the old man related.

The old fellow had no ax to grind in any of this. No reason whatsoever either to lie or even to gild the lily a bit. He wasn't going to get any more money by making the tale more interesting than it already was. So Longarm pretty much had to assume that he was telling it straight.

And the straight version of this, the one Ignacio Fernandez apparently did not want Longarm to know, was that these two shooters were *insurrectes*—if Longarm had the word right—rebels, in any event, who were part of the current effort by one bunch of assholes to wrest power from the governing bunch of assholes, so the new crop could be the ones to steal from the peons and the taxpayers.

Longarm didn't make any attempt to keep up with Mexican politics, but it seemed there was always somebody whipping up a rebellion to topple whoever was governing at that particular moment.

And the two shooters were part of this latest movement to overthrow the government and install a new one.

Longarm had questioned the old man at length about that point, if only because it made so little sense.

"Oh yes, *senor*. The things this man said to you before the authorities arrived, he was very unhappy with you, *senor*. I heard these things while he was lying there. He cursed you, *senor*, but not for his pain. He is a dead man. He knows this when he falls. He accepts his death."

Longarm figured that to be sheer exaggeration. The guy was only shot in the legs. He wasn't going to croak just from that.

"His anger is that you live. His anger is that because of this, because of you, the revolution is delayed."

Longarm could only shake his head when the old man said that. "Friend, I don't know nor, t' tell you the truth, care about this revolution thing. It's got nothing t' do with me."

"But this is what he says, *senor*. Several times this man is in grief because he has failed to kill you; several times he says now the revolution is in jep . . . jep . . ."

"Jeopardy?"

"Ah. Thank you. That is the word, yes. Jeopardy. Several times he says the revolution is now in jeopardy."

"Because he didn't kill me? You're sure that's what he meant?"

"Oh yes, *senor*. It was most clear."

"That doesn't make sense," Longarm mused aloud. "I don't even know who these people are or what they want. An' I've sure never done anything that would affect them one way or t'other."

"I can only say to you what the injured man said while he was in pain. The words were clear. What is behind them. . . ." The elderly gent spread his hands and shrugged. "This I do not know."

"Me neither," Longarm said.

Longarm sat and chewed on that information for a considerable time after the old fellow accepted his payment with dignity and left the cafe. Longarm overpaid him outrageously, but what the hell? He and Henry between them would surely be able to work out some way to get it approved for reimbursement when the expense voucher was filed.

No sir, he finally decided. This revolution stuff made no sense whatsoever. Longarm had nothing to do with that and damn sure didn't want anything to do with it, either.

All he wanted was to get Adolph Jurneman in custody and take the son of a bitch back to Denver for trial.

And that, dammit, he intended to pursue again right now, while Nacho Fernandez was on duty. Seemed such occasions were almighty rare, and Longarm didn't want to let this one pass by.

He paid for his meal and headed back toward city hall.

"What d'you mean he isn't here? I saw him not more than an hour ago. I told him I'd be coming in."

"I am sorry, *senor*." This was yet another person on duty, this one a civilian or at least someone not in uniform. The good news was that his English was excellent.

The civilian smiled warmly. He seemed genuinely interested in trying to help. "You are of course aware that this is not the normal place of duty for Captain Fernandez?"

"But I thought . . ." Longarm clamped his jaw hard shut. "No. I didn't know that."

"You could inquire at the military barracks."

"And that would be where?" Longarm asked.

"In the block behind this building, *senor*."

"I see. And do you know anything about a prisoner? An American named Adolph Jurneman?"

"I know this man is in custody, *senor*. I know he is to be transferred to the American authorities immediately upon presentation of the necessary papers."

Longarm's eyebrows went up and probably his blood pressure did, too. "Mister, I *am* the American authority Jurneman's t' be turned over to, and I already gave those papers to Captain Fernandez. Days ago."

"About this, *senor*, I know nothing."

"He put the papers in that file drawer right over there," Longarm said, pointing.

"I would not know about this, sir."

"Would you look in there an' see if everything's in order so I can take my prisoner and go? Please?"

The civilian shrugged and rose. He pulled the drawer open and picked through the folders stored there. "I am sorry, *senor*. There is nothing."

"What about the ledger? I saw him make a notation in a ledger book. He took that out of a drawer down there." Again, Longarm pointed, this time to the reception desk.

"Very well, *senor*." The gentleman smiled. "We shall see, eh?"

They saw. The ledger book was right there. The civilian government employee opened it to the date Longarm indicated. Ran his finger down the correct page. "I see here, *senor*, where Captain Fernandez signed himself onto duty that morning. The next entry shows that the captain signed out to return to the army barracks." He shrugged. "There is nothing else written in his hand, *senor*. Nor is there anything about the visit you say you made here."

"But he got out the red ink and stamped the extradition paper and signed it and . . . there's nothing about the extradition in that book, is there?"

"No, *senor*. There is not."

"I think," Longarm said, with a display of calm that he did not feel, "I think I should go make some inquiries of Captain Fernandez."

"You should find him at the barracks. He is the provost there."

"Friend, you've been a bigger help to me than you may realize. Thank you very much."

"Any time, *senor*. Any time."

Longarm's expression was grim when he left the Del Norte city hall.

131

Chapter 31

They had to scour through half the administrative offices in the place before they finally found someone who spoke English well enough to handle the needed translations. When one was located he introduced himself.

"*Senor*, I am Lieutenant Pablo Martine. This officer," he inclined his head toward the beribboned and mustachioed man beside him, "is our *commandante* Major Eduardo Rivera."

Longarm returned the favor and shook hands with both men, then presented his credentials for their inspection before he explained the problem. "Looks now like the extradition paper can't be found," he said at length. "It was signed by your ambassador and our attorney general, an' the whole thing seemed clear enough until the document went missing. I think we need t' ask Captain Fernandez what's happened to it so the transfer can be arranged.

"An' once we've done that, which is the official part of my reason for being here, I'd very much like to interrogate the wounded rebel who tried to shoot me a little while ago." Longarm bowed slightly in the direction of the major. "With your permission, of course."

Martine and Rivera exchanged some comments back and forth, the junior officer apparently delivering as much information as he was getting instruction back. Eventually he turned to Longarm with the outcome of the conversation.

"We find ourselves in a position of great embarrassment, *Senor* Long," Martine said.

"How's that, Lieutenant?"

"Our Captain Fernandez is not at his post of duty."

"But I saw him just this morning. He was leading a squad of soldiers at the scene of the shooting."

"So I am aware, *senor*. The captain did return to the barracks with this detachment, just as you say. Unfortunately the captain left almost immediately thereafter, even though he was under orders to report to the major. He failed to do so. We have been . . . looking for him since that time."

"And the extradition paper?"

Lieutenant Martine shrugged. "Of this we do not know. The commandante has been told nothing about this paper you say you delivered."

"I gave it to Fernandez. He's had it for days. He kept leaving word he was working on the release."

"You say he left word? With whom?"

Longarm told him.

"We will, of course, verify this that you say."

"Yes. Please."

The lieutenant conversed again with the major, who scowled ferociously and with a bellow brought a sergeant and three corporals on the run. The sergeant was given orders, snapped off a salute and spun about to leave at quick-time while the corporals returned to whatever it was they'd been doing.

"Inquiries are being made," Martine said unnecessarily.

"Yeah. So I gathered. Is there any chance I can go ahead an' take custody of my prisoner now? You obviously already were alerted to the transfer by your Foreign Office. And those messages Fernandez left for me will confirm that I did present the paperwork even if it's missing now."

"Yes, *Senor* Long, but . . ." Martine looked very upset.

"Sentences that start with the words 'Yes, but' aren't generally very pleasant ones t' hear, Lieutenant."

"Nor will this one be, *senor*. The embarrassment I spoke of extends to more than the disappearance of Captain Fernandez from his post."

Longarm waited for the blow to fall.

"The prisoner Hurneman . . ." the pronunciation seemed odd to an English speaker but there was no doubt about the meaning.

"Yes?"

Martine glanced toward the major, then braced himself and returned his attention to the American visitor.

"The prisoner has been released, *senor*."

"Re . . . !"

"On bail, *senor*."

"Bail? That's impossible. He. . . ."

"There was an error in the paperwork, *senor*."

"I don't suppose that paperwork came under Captain Fernandez's control?" Longarm speculated.

"Sadly, *senor*, I must tell you that, indeed, it was."

"I see. And, um, just when was it that this happened?" Longarm thought he already knew the answer to that one. But he wanted to hear it from the Mexican authorities anyway.

"This morning, *senor*."

"After Fernandez returned with the fellow I shot?" Longarm guessed.

"*Si.*"

"Then I need t' speak with him all the more, Lieutenant. Would you be willing to handle the translation for me? I'm pretty sure from the way the man acted this morning that he doesn't have any more English than I have Spanish. An' about all I can say in Spanish is *cervesa*."

"You very well may want something stronger than a beer, *senor*, when I tell you that it will not be possible for you to interview this man."

"Now look, Lieutenant, I. . . ."

"Please, *senor*. It is not that we are unwilling. We are unable."

"He got out on bond too, did he?"

"No, *senor*. He is dead."

"But I only shot him in the legs, dammit. He didn't bleed all that much an' neither one o' those wounds was life threatening."

"I am sorry, *senor*. I know only that the man who shot at you was taken to the jail infirmary. A doctor was summoned. When he arrived, the prisoner was dead. I do not, at this moment, know how he died. News of this death arrived shortly before you did, *senor*. I assumed he died of his wounds and inquired no further attention. Now . . ." Martine turned and spoke at length again with the major.

"Inquiries will be made," he said when he and the major were done with this conversation.

"I don't suppose Captain Fernandez was alone with the fellow for any length of time after he was taken to your infirmary?" Longarm asked.

"That too will be looked into, *senor*."

"So I got no federal prisoner to take across the border and you got no captain or wounded rebel to interrogate."

"That would seem to be the case, yes." Lieutenant Martine sounded both sad and embarrassed. But then, Longarm thought, he damned well ought to be both of those things. Behind him the major looked so downcast Longarm thought his mustache had begun to droop.

"Helluva day in Del Norte, huh?"

"I would have to agree, *Senor* Long. For what it is worth, I am sorry. As is Major Rivera."

135

"Yeah. Sure." Longarm sighed. There was not a damned thing he could do about any of it, of course. And there would be no point at all in berating these Mexican officers. They'd apologized. He was sure they meant it. At this point that was just about all any of them could do. Express regret. And move on.

Longarm thanked them for their time and help. "If you learn anything, I would appreciate bein' notified." He told them where he was staying on the El Paso side and thanked them again, offering his hand first to Major Rivera and then to Lieutenant Martine.

After that he got the hell out of the barracks and, as quickly as he could manage it, out of Del Norte as well.

This time no one tried to ambush him on his way back to the American side of the border.

Chapter 32

Carlton was awake when Longarm checked on him in the downslope of the afternoon. He was weak and groggy, but his eyes were open and he seemed to understand where he was and what was happening. When Longarm got there Anita was patiently and very carefully spooning chicken broth into Carlton, a few scant drops at a time.

Anita paused in her ministrations only long enough to give Longarm a cheerful smile before she went back to blowing on the soup to cool it and then dribbling it past Carlton's lips.

Carlton turned his head to see who'd come in and a trickle of soup, yellow with chicken fat, ran out of the corner of his mouth. Anita picked up a cloth and sopped up the liquid before it could reach Carlton's neck.

"You look like shit," Longarm said.

Carlton gave him a wan smile and a wink.

"Feel like it too, don't you?"

The wounded man nodded.

"Yeah, well, that'll go away. Looks to me like you're in pretty good hands here."

Carlton nodded again.

"I'll look in on you again t'morrow morning."

Carlton raised an eyebrow.

"I'll explain everything then. Right now, old friend, I'm tired an' hungry an' out of sorts. Is that okay by you?"

Carlton nodded.

"Is there anything I can get you, Anita? You want me to send somebody in to take over here so you can get some rest?"

She gave him a dirty look and a cussing out in Spanish.

"That's a firm no, huh?"

Anita sniffed and tossed her head, her glossy mane of hair flying. Then she fed Carlton another few drops of broth.

Longarm was smiling when he left Jim Quayne's office. He'd for sure expected Carlton to be dead by now. Instead, it looked . . . well, it was too soon to say that. But it sure looked like he might make it through.

He thought about walking over to the restaurant where they served such tender steak—the memory of that slab of overaged bull wasn't easy to forget, but the follow-up had been good enough—then turned instead toward the Torres's cafe. He wanted to talk as well as to eat, and he could count on the Torreses to give him straight answers.

"The revolutionaries, *senor*?" Torres looked sad. "What can I tell you? They are people who make grand promises. All revolutionaries do this. Then they either die or they become the government, no? If they die, the first government is cruel and takes everything from the peon through taxes and laws to favor the rich. If the revolutionaries succeed and become the government, *senor*, then *they* take everything from the peon with more taxes and even more laws to favor the rich. It has always been so, *senor*. It will not change with these men."

"Do you know who they are?" Longarm asked.

"I do not know these men. I have not wanted to know

them. For you, *senor* . . . would you like me to ask about them?"

"Yes, *Senor* Torres. I would appreciate that very much. Now there's one more favor I would ask of you."

"Anything, *senor*. You have my word on this. If it is within my power, this thing shall be yours."

"Good," Longarm declared. "An' what I'd like is one of your wife's fine meals but only if you'll let me pay for it."

"*Senor*, please, I. . . ."

"You gave me your word, y'know."

Torres sighed. "Yes, *senor*. As you wish."

Longarm sat back and gave some attention to the coffee cup in front of him.

"Marshal Long."

"Yes, John?" He turned away from the stairs and headed instead for the hotel desk where the night manager was motioning for him.

John dropped his voice to a hoarse whisper and mumbled something, Longarm had no idea what.

"I'm sorry. I couldn't hear that."

Only a trifle louder John said, "You have a visitor, Marshal. In the dining room."

"Who?"

"I don't know her name, Marshal."

Her? A woman? The only female he knew on either side of the border was Anita, and she would still be busy nursing Carlton back to health. Still . . . He passed through the wide doorway that connected the hotel lobby with the dining room.

"Miss . . . ," he had to think hard to remember it, "Miss Everly, isn't it?"

"Yes, Marshal, it is."

This time she knew the difference between a policeman and a federal deputy, he noted.

"The gentleman at the desk said you're waiting to see me?"

"That is correct, sir."

"May I?" He reached for the back of one of the chairs at the table where she'd apparently just finished her supper.

"Could we speak somewhere more private? Please?"

Longarm looked around. There were only three other people there and they were halfway across the big room. They couldn't possibly have overheard anything said at this table unless Longarm and Miss Everly were deliberately loud in their conversation. "Certainly," he said. "Wherever you wish."

He had, however, some unspoken reservations. If she wanted him to accompany her into a darkened alley, well, something like that was not apt to happen.

"Could we go to your room, Marshal?"

"Sure." He helped her with her chair and waited while she gathered up a velveteen purse, an ivory-colored knitted wrap and a pale blue parasol.

She was, he noted, a mighty fine figure of a woman. This evening she was wearing another high-neck, long-sleeve shirtwaist and a heavy skirt cinched tight around a waist that seemed quite impossibly small. She wore a carved ivory cameo attached to a black ribbon tied at her throat, just barely visible above the lace of her high-buttoned collar.

Between waist and throat were those bold, firm, magnificent tits. But he was on duty here and should remember to act as a reasonable approximation of a gentleman. He refrained from making any vulgar remarks or reaching out and milking one of those boobs. He was tempted toward both.

Instead, he only bowed and followed her meekly out of the dining room and through the lobby to the stairs.

It was just a damned shame, he thought, that what John

would be thinking right now would not be accurate. This full-bodied filly was one a man would want to keep his chaps and spurs on for, so he could give her a wilder ride without bucking off.

Chapter 33

Miss Everly was one extra fine-looking woman. But she did work for a man whose power and finances were both tied to the shady side of El Paso—a blatantly impossible figure of speech, that; it generally seemed to him that there was no actual shade in El Paso—and Lord knew what that could imply.

For sure, Longarm was not going to rely on the lady's innocence and virtue to protect him. When he opened that hotel room door he was not standing in front of it, nor was he the first to walk into the room. Just in case.

As it happened, there was no would-be assassin lurking inside. He looked.

"Are you always this cautious?" Miss Everly asked after Longarm had thoroughly searched the place, including inside the wardrobe and outside the window too.

"Yes, I am," he told her. Which was almost true. Call it a mild exaggeration, rather than a lie.

"Are you quite finished now?"

He nodded.

The lady gave him a look—chin low, eyes speculative—that he could not quite read. Then she walked over to the door, which he'd left standing open as a matter of

142

course, that being the customary method of protecting a woman's reputation if she were alone with a gentleman who was not her husband.

Miss Everly closed the door, careful to let the latch click fully shut. Then, she slid the bolt in place to lock it. No one could intrude even if they had a key.

She turned. Lifted her chin. This time he had no trouble at all reading her expression. It was imperious. Challenging. Haughty.

She stripped off her gloves. Tossed them and her handbag onto the one chair in the place.

Longarm took a cheroot from his coat pocket and got out a penknife to trim it with.

"I have a message for you," Miss Everly said.

"All right."

She reached around to her side—stupid place to put buttons, he'd always thought—and unfastened the skirt. She let it slide to the floor, exposing legs that were good. A trifle heavy in the thighs, perhaps, but overall quite nice. And she wasn't wearing stockings. Beneath the skirt she was bare-legged. Not that he blamed her in the El Paso heat.

Longarm brought out a match and thumbed it aflame, using it to slowly warm the barrel of the cheroot while taking care not to scorch the outer leaf. It was a process that required some concentration.

"You must earn what I have to tell you," Miss Everly said as she slipped out of her shirtwaist and dropped it onto the chair along with her purse and gloves. Her voice, Longarm thought, was a mite irritated.

"How's that?" he asked, but only when he was quite done with the cheroot. The match had burned low so he shook it out and flicked it into a corner. He dipped two fingers into his vest pocket and found another match.

"Look at *me!*" Miss Everly snapped. "Not at that damned cigar."

Longarm glanced in her direction. She was wearing a chemise, shoes and the cameo. Nothing else at this point.

She quickly slipped the chemise over her head and threw it onto the chair. Now there were the shoes and the cameo at the throat and nothing in between.

She had a body that a sculptor would die for. Or a saloon wall painter. Absolutely magnificent jugs. Tiny waist so small she must surely be originally from the south where women were known to have ribs removed so they could achieve waists like that.

He still thought, though, that her thighs were a little too heavy. And her ass was kinda wide. The size of her tits served to balance that. But even so. Longarm would have preferred sleeker hips and butt.

He lighted the second match, stuck the cheroot between his teeth and bent his head to meet the match flame.

"I *said*," she said, "you have to earn the message. Now come *here!*"

She planted her feet wide apart. Forgot for a moment that the skirt was still around her ankles and damn near tripped herself.

Longarm managed to avoid laughing out loud, but he wouldn't have been a bit surprised if his eyes gave him away.

For her part, Miss Everly looked pissed off—at herself and the offending skirt. She stamped her foot a little too loudly when she kicked the skirt out of her way.

But she quickly recovered her aplomb. And her haughty, demanding demeanor. She cupped her bush like a man cupping his balls and said, "Eat this. Do what I say."

Longarm snorted. And finished lighting his cheroot.

He shook out the flame of the second match and tossed it aside, too. With the cigar still between his teeth and his head canted slightly to one side so the smoke rising off the cheroot would not lift into his eyes he said, "Fuck you, lady."

"*Damn* you!"

"Lady, you're playing a game here. Thing is, it takes two for most games."

"I won't tell you what the message is if you don't do what I say."

"Now there's a threat, all right. Lady, I know who you work for. The message has t' come from him. If you don't wanta tell me, fine. Tomorrow I'll go ask the son of a bitch. In the meantime, if you want to get laid, that's okay by me. Say so and I'll nail you to this floor. But don't think you're gonna walk in here and play mistress of the manor with me for your whipping boy. That's a game I don't play very well, so if we're gonna make the beast with two backs, I'll be the one on top. Understand that or take your temper tantrum someplace else."

He took the cheroot out of his mouth and spent some time looking her over while she stood there hovering between seething anger and acute embarrassment. He could see the telltale blush start on her chest and rise onto her throat and cheeks.

"Now," he said patiently, his voice calm and pleasant. "Would you like to fuck or not?" He smiled at her.

She tried to maintain an air of control. But it didn't work. After only a few seconds her eyes shifted away from his and she nodded. "Yes," she whispered.

"I'm sorry. I didn't hear you." He had, of course. But what the hell.

"Yes."

"Yes, what?"

"Yes, I would like you to fuck me."

"And how d'you ask?"

"Please," she whispered.

"All right then. Get on the bed an' I'll be with you soon as I finish this smoke. An' mind you take your shoes off first. I don't want you dragging any mud into my bed."

"Yes, sir." She sounded thoroughly chastened. But she looked quite thoroughly aroused. Her nipples—smaller than he would have expected on tits that big and so pale it was hard to see where her areolae began—had become as engorged and erect as a pair of small peckers. And he could see moisture glistening on the lips of her pussy, which looked pink and eager inside its nest of dark, curly pubic hair.

Longarm gathered that yeah, he'd read her right. She demanded control. But what this one truly wanted was to be controlled. She had the appearance of being in charge of things, but she wanted a man to dominate her.

Fine. That was a desire he reckoned he could accommodate.

As for himself, well, maybe he wasn't quite as disinterested as he wanted the lady to believe. He was able to finish his smoke and get out of his clothes in damn near record time.

Chapter 34

T. Wade Kaufman would like to speak with him. That was the extent of the not-so-mysterious message Zoe Everly delivered. Then, exhausted, sweaty and her breath smelling of cum, she kissed him inside the privacy of the hotel room and allowed Longarm to walk her home as a gentleman right properly should.

He went back to the hotel and slept the sleep of the just. Or, if not exactly the just, then the sleep of exhaustion. Miss Everly had proven to be a handful. In the morning, he slept later than usual, so he found a cab and took it to the Kaufman building after a quick breakfast in the hotel.

"Yes, sir? May I help you?" Zoe acted like she'd never seen him before in her life.

"Deputy Long to see Mr. Kaufman, please."

"Yes, sir." She reached under her desk and did something—pulled a bell cord would be his guess—and seconds later, a young man, with slicked down hair and a suit that was probably older than he was, showed up to act as escort. "Please take the marshal to see Mr. Kaufman, Albert."

"Yes, miss." The boy looked like he was hopelessly in

love with Zoe, which she pretended not to notice. Longarm wondered if he should clue the kid in. Ignore the lady, insult her, maybe slap her a few times and she'd come around and make like a tigress.

"Reading law under Mr. Kaufman are you?" Longarm asked as they walked down the corridor.

"Yes, sir." Albert beamed. "It's a privilege."

"Uh huh." Longarm had his own opinions about that, but he had no intention of trying to disillusion the young man. That would come in its own good time.

"In here, sir. And would you care for anything? Coffee perhaps?"

"No, thanks. I'm fine."

Albert opened the door and shepherded Longarm inside.

Wade Kaufman was in the process of dictating something to an exceptionally handsome middle-aged woman. "Come in, Longarm. We'll pick this up again later, Bessie, thank you."

The amanuensis gathered her notepads and pencils and nodded to Longarm on her way out. She gently closed the door as she left.

"Got your message," Longarm said. "What can I do for you?"

"The question is, what can I do for you?" Kaufman said.

"How's that?"

"I believe I told you that your situation made me curious and that I intended to look into it."

"I remember."

"Yes, well, I've made inquiries. I thought you might be interested in the answers that were obtained. Sit down, Longarm. Please. Can I offer you anything? A drink? Something to eat perhaps?"

Longarm took the seat, but declined the snack. Kaufman tugged a bell cord and Albert instantly showed up. "Coffee, son, and a tray of pastries."

:"Yes, sir." Albert withdrew, and Kaufman returned his attention to Longarm, who lighted a cheroot and waited.

"You may be aware that there is a revolution brewing on the other side of the river," Kaufman said.

"Yes, of course."

"Revolutions require certain things if they are to proceed. Money comes immediately to mind, of course."

That wasn't the first thing Longarm thought of when the topic of revolution came up. Justice, freedom, oppression, that was the sort of thing he might think of before the subject of money occurred to him. But then he wasn't in quite the same position that Kaufman was either, and his perspective was bound to be different.

"I am reliably told," Kaufman said, "that this revolution is well-financed. They say it is an uprising of the people. That, of course, is complete bullshit. There have been such things as populist uprisings in the course of human history. But not well-funded movements as this one seems to be. Someone . . . I will tell you honestly that I do not yet know who . . . is subsidizing this revolution. It stands to reason that whoever this benefactor is, he intends to personally gain from any success. And the fact that he is being very careful to remain anonymous suggests to me that he wants to be careful to suffer no damage beyond monetary inconvenience should the revolution fail. Do you follow me?"

"Clear enough," Longarm said, "though I can't see why I should care about any of it."

"You should if you care who it is who wants you dead," Kaufman said.

"Me? That doesn't make sense. I don't give a fat rat's ass what happens to the politics over there."

"Perhaps not, but they seem to care about you. Or did. After Miss Everly left here yesterday evening to deliver her message to you, I received additional word suggesting—mind, this is not confirmed—suggesting that the interest in your death may be waning now for reason or reasons unknown to me. Something seems to have happened yesterday that made your demise unnecessary."

Longarm grunted. That made as little sense to him as the rest of it did, and he said so.

Albert returned with a carafe of coffee and a silver tray laden with crullers, fruit-filled turnovers and a layered pastry that seemed to be covered with ground nuts and honey.

"Are you sure you won't join me?"

"No, thank you."

"That will be all, Albert."

"Yes, sir."

"Where were we?" Kaufman asked around a mouthful of sugar and flaky dough.

"Across the border. D'you think they could've gotten discouraged because I killed a couple of them yesterday?" Longarm asked.

"I heard about that, but I do not think it would have been significant. If it were to change anything, I would think it would increase their desire to see you dead, not eliminate it. Those dead men were only peons. Thoroughly expendable."

Kaufman reached for one of the honey-covered pastries and popped it into his mouth whole, then licked the honey from his fingers. "Baklava. It's Greek. Really quite good." He smiled. "Not tempted?"

"I just had breakfast," Longarm explained. Kaufman probably had, too. But then Kaufman probably weighed three times what Longarm did.

"It puzzles me, Longarm, but there you have it. At some point yesterday it became unnecessary for you to die."

"It had nothing t' do with Ronny Worrell then," Longarm said.

"No. The orders and the bankroll for your murder definitely came from the Mexican side of the border, specifically from the revolutionary movement."

"Would've been convenient if it was Worrell. Easy to take him down. Might not be so simple to bust up a whole revolution though."

"Personal retribution, Longarm? That surprises me. I would have thought you would simply complete your business here and return to Colorado. It, uh, it is Denver where you're based, is it not?"

"You heard right about that. But it looks like I won't be heading home any time soon. Seems the fellow I was supposed to take back under an extradition order was turned loose by a captain who's also gone missing."

"Ah, yes. That would be Nacho Fernandez. I heard he scampered for some reason. I shall miss him."

"You'll miss Fernandez?"

Kaufman smiled. "Not for personal reasons, you understand. He was very useful to me however. And not terribly expensive considering the results his position allowed him to obtain."

"I see." Longarm sighed. "If I'd known that early enough I would've bribed the son of a bitch in time to get Adolph Jurneman out of that Mexican jail and into my custody."

"You were here to collect Adolph?" Kaufman asked.

"That's right. You know him?"

"I did not say that."

"No, I expect you didn't at that."

"Please keep that clear in your mind."

"It's clear," Longarm said.

"Thank you." Kaufman sat back and steepled his fingers, peering inside the fleshy structure as if seeking inspiration. After a few moments he leaned forward, took another pastry off the tray and munched on it absently while he continued to think.

"You may . . ." Kaufman said, after a fairly considerable period has passed, "you may have just discovered your link with the revolutionaries."

"How's that?" Longarm asked.

"There is a rumor—and please note that I am acting in full cooperation with you . . . there is a rumor that Adolph came here with a rather large cargo of goods that he placed for sale. Only a rumor, of course."

"Goods," Longarm repeated. "And, uh, what might those goods be?"

"Please understand that as an officer of the court, I would harbor no information about illicit merchandise," Kaufman said.

Longarm was puzzled. Again. "What the hell would be illegal to sell across the border into Mexico? Who would care?"

"I have no idea," Kaufman said.

Longarm was certain the man was lying. He knew much more than he was saying but had his own reasons to avoid admitting anything about Adolph Jurneman's cargo to a deputy United States marshal.

Still and all, dammit, Longarm could not think of a single sort of merchandise that would be illegal if transported into Mexico.

Guns? That thought was natural enough considering that there were revolutionaries involved in this.

But hell, a man could buy, transport and sell weapons by the trainload if he pleased. He might want to keep the Mexican authorities from knowing about it, but nobody on the American side would give a shit.

Longarm shook his head. "You aren't helping me very much."

"I am helping you more than I really should." Kaufman poured a fresh cup of coffee and used it to dunk doughnuts into.

Longarm hadn't been much tempted by the Greek thing, whatever it was, but there is something about a doughnut dunked in hot coffee that is almighty appealing. He ignored the very small urge to indulge and asked, "Is there anything else you can tell me?"

Kaufman permitted himself a smile. "Can, do you ask? Or will?"

Longarm laughed. "Lemme rephrase that then. Is there anything else you will tell me?"

"No. I've said too much already."

"Any idea where I can find Adolph Jurneman?"

Kaufman hesitated. Then he shook his head. "Sorry."

He knew, dammit. Kaufman knew where Jurneman was. Or anyway knew something that would lead to him. But that was not knowledge he was willing to share with a lawman.

"You've been very kind," Longarm said, meaning it. Kaufman had told him more than he'd expected to learn from a crooked lawyer.

"Do remember that for future reference," Kaufman suggested.

"I'll not only remember it myself," Longarm said, "I'll pass it along t' somebody else down this way if I can."

Kaufman smiled again. This was quite obviously what he'd hoped for. And it was a perfectly fair exchange, Longarm figured. You help me; I help you; everybody's happy in the long run.

Longarm thanked Kaufman and, on his way out, motioned for the amanuensis to return to the office. He paused at Zoe Everly's desk and lowered his voice so the several men waiting in the lobby could not overhear. "Tonight," he said. "Seven o'clock at my room. Don't be wearin' anything under your skirt. Nothing at all, hear."

Zoe acted like she hadn't heard.

Chapter 35

"Good morning." Longarm could hardly believe the improvement he saw in Carlton. His old friend was awake and even looked cheerful. His color was much improved too.

"Hello yourself." Carlton's voice was strong too. Far from normal but certainly firm enough.

At this point, it was Anita who looked the worse off. But then she hadn't been to bed in days, nor had she left Carlton's side long enough to go fetch a change of clothing.

Longarm took her by the arms and bent his head close to hers. "Why don't you go wash and get yourself something to eat," he said gently.

"Oh no, *senor.* I would not leave him so long. But . . . I would like to go to the outhouse. Would you stay with him for just a few minutes? Please, *senor?*"

"I'll be right here." The words sounded normal. He hoped. But. . . .

He turned to Carlton and asked, "Where's the doctor?"

"He went out yesterday afternoon. Some woman having trouble with a birthing. He hasn't been back since."

Longarm glanced toward the door, in the direction Anita just went, and said, "Jim hasn't been here since yesterday? But I thought . . ."

"Go ahead. Spit it out."

"All right, dammit. I thought I smelled something on her breath just now."

Carlton cackled. "For a fact."

"Jesus, Carlton, in your condition?"

"She was just trying to comfort me. Keep me interested in living and getting well, like. It worked better'n either one of us thought it could."

"But you shouldn't ought to be humping up an' down like that," Longarm warned.

"Didn't have to. Just laid there and didn't move. Anita, she did all the rest. I tell you, Longarm, that girl is a comfort to an old man." He laughed again. "More so than I ever expected. I owe you for this, you know. Owe you plenty."

"You don't owe me a damn thing. I'm just happy for you, that's all."

"I'm surprised you're still here," Carlton said. "Thought you'd have had your man and been gone long since."

Longarm filled him in on what had happened.

Carlton whistled. "Nacho abandoned his commission and ran off with the revolutionaries? That's serious."

"I wouldn't care about that except for him taking Jurneman with him. Which reminds me. Wade Kaufman said Jurneman had something that he wanted to sell to the revolutionaries and that might be why they wanted me out of the way an' Jurneman out of jail. Any idea what that could be about?"

"I hadn't heard anything like that," Carlton said.

"Would you have?"

"Maybe. Maybe not. I would've heard everything the Mexican authorities knew. I have good contacts there. But

155

beyond that I can't be so sure. Did you say something about a cargo of goods though?"

Longarm nodded.

"Still on this side of the border."

"Far as I know, yes. Unless Jurneman struck his deal and moved the stuff over last night."

"Moved what stuff?" Anita asked. She returned in time to hear the last few sentences but no more than that.

Longarm explained the situation to her.

"Guns," she said firmly.

"I don't think so. We're looking for something illegal. There's nothing illegal about selling guns to a Mexican citizen."

"Guns," she insisted. "A man that I . . . entertained . . ." she blushed and gave Carlton a look of apology.

"It's all right, dear," he assured her. "Go on. What did you hear?"

"A week ago. Maybe more, maybe less, I don' remember. He said that guns will be bought. This man . . . he was one of them. He was proud. Bragging. He said an American would sell them."

"But why would they be illegal?" Longarm asked. "On this side, I mean?"

Anita shrugged. "I do not understand all the man said. I was not listening so much. You know?"

"Anything you can remember would be a big help," Longarm told her.

"Please," Carlton added. His one word seemed to have more weight with her than a thousand pleas from Longarm could have.

Anita gave Carlton an anxious look, then said, "Special guns. Something about them is special. I don' know what."

"Special guns," Longarm repeated. What the hell would make one gun any more special than another? Repeating

156

rifles? There was nothing special about that nowadays. And they would not be illegal in any case.

Anita thought for a moment, then brightened and said, "I do not know about these guns, *senor*. But would it be of service to know where you would find them?"

"Jeez, yes," Longarm blurted. "Please."

Chapter 36

Hindsight always gives such a perfect look at things, Longarm reminded himself. He'd come off from Denver with his saddle—which he hadn't needed and probably wouldn't—but without his Winchester. Which he sure as hell would've liked to have in his hand right now. The firepower in his Colt was limited, and there was no telling what he might be going up against.

If anything.

He could hope the warehouse would be empty except for Jurneman's crates of 'special' guns of whatever sort. Then he could get the lay of things and decide afterward how to handle a stakeout and arrest.

He wasn't going to count on that, though. Wasn't going to turn to the El Paso police, either. Wouldn't that be a waste of time?

He would have trusted the Texas Rangers to back him up any day of the week. But he had no idea where the nearest Rangers were working at the moment and doubted he had time to be sending requests for assistance to their headquarters in Austin, then waiting around for replies and reinforcement.

No, damn it, it looked like he was going to have to handle this alone.

Just to be on the safe side, though, he borrowed an idea from the revolutionaries' own book and armed himself with a shotgun in addition to his familiar Colt.

One of the sawed-off scatterguns that his would-be assassins used would've been just fine. Except he did not happen to have one of those. He settled for asking Torres for the loan of a shotgun if he had one.

Torres did own a shotgun. Once he saw it, Longarm almost wished the restaurant owner didn't.

Sawed off? When the butt of this clunky old thing was resting on the ground, the sonuvabitch was so long-barreled the muzzles reached close to shoulder high. And it was heavy enough that it should've been mounted on a caisson.

Torres used it in winter, he said, when the ducks and geese were rafting on the slow-moving waters of the Rio Grande.

On the up side of things, the big old shoulder cannon was of 10 gauge so it carried several ounces of shot in each shell. Those long barrels also reached out to distances usually suitable only for rifle fire.

Torres offered Longarm his half box of Number 2 shot to go with the gun, but Longarm declined that suggestion. Instead, he stopped at a hardware store and picked up a full box of Single Ought buckshot.

Thus armed he figured he could take on grizzly bears, circus lions or a squadron of Mexican revolutionaries. If he had to.

Anita's directions took him south along the river to a crumbling and seemingly deserted bodega that had seen better days. The warehouse sat on a low bluff overlooking the Rio Grande. Longarm couldn't help but notice that there was a path worn into the bluff descending from the warehouse to the water's edge. And on the far side of the river there was a matching path leading into Mexico.

When Longarm arrived, it was in mid-afternoon, and he gathered that he was barely in time to find out what this was all about and, hopefully, to arrest Adolph Jurneman as well.

Over on the Chihuahua side he could see four freight wagons parked. That might or might not be normal. He couldn't be sure about that. But he was damned well certain that Mexican freight wagons are not normally pulled by teams of sleek, fat and handsome Belgian draft horses. There were four horses to the hitch and every one of them looked as fancy as anything you might see pulling a brewing company's show-off rig.

That, he thought, was considerably out of the ordinary.

Down at river level things did not seem normal either. Someone had a temporary ferry in place there. Laboriously and sturdily-erected pilings had been set in place to anchor a thick hawser to which was attached a crudely-built raft. Lighter lines connected to the pilings would no doubt serve to pull the raft back and forth and thereby ferry goods from the U.S. into Mexico.

Judging from the hasty quality of construction on that raft, Longarm figured the ferry would be cut loose and abandoned once the goods were across.

He also would have placed plenty on a wager that for whatever reason this warehouse and this temporary crossing were not being used for the first time.

Longarm didn't much care what might have been smuggled through here before. But if Adolph Jurneman was involved . . . now that interested him plenty.

There was no sign of people outside the warehouse. That did not, however, mean the place was empty. That ferry on the river and those wagons on the other side were not there merely to kill time.

Longarm double-checked the gleaming brass shotshells

in the breech of Torres's 10 gauge. Then he felt to make sure the Colt was loose in its holster and tossed the stub of a cheroot aside before he walked soft and silent into the adobe-walled corral at the rear of the old bodega.

Chapter 37

My oh my, what *do* we have here? Longarm silently wondered.

Workmen. Each loaded with crates that must've been damn-all heavy judging by the way the Mexicans carried them. He saw four men paired up two to the crate and even so the weight looked to be about as much as they could handle and just a wee bit more. The lifting and carrying was obviously a struggle.

The workmen came out of the wide double doors at the rear of the bodega, muscling the crates into the sunshine and across the empty corral toward a gate that would lead them onto the path and down to the waiting ferry. Apparently they were only now beginning to load Jurneman's special cargo for transport across the river.

Longarm could not see Jurneman. For that matter he never had seen the fugitive. He had descriptions of him, but that was all.

The Mexicans and their burden proceeded across the corral toward Longarm who was standing in plain sight beside the gate, the huge old goose gun resting butt down on the ground.

Longarm touched the brim of his hat as the men came near and gave them a cheerful hello.

"Que?"

"Quien es?"

"Mind if I take a look at those crates, gentlemen?" Never mind that none of them seemed to understand a word he was saying. He'd asked the question nice and proper, and that is what he would testify to in a court of law if it came to that.

The Mexicans started to talk among themselves. One pair set their crate down and gestured for the other two to do the same. The one who was taking charge said something and turned to go back to the warehouse.

"Hold it!" Longarm said sharply.

And then he did something that in retrospect was probably kind of dumb. He pulled out his wallet and displayed his badge.

The effect was something on the order of taking a hard kick at a tall ant hill.

And these ants had something better than stingers. They had pistols, which they were damned quick to produce.

The leader snatched a small revolver from his waistband.

Longarm was slowed by having to transfer the shotgun from one hand to the other, and the Mexican's gun was in his hand before Longarm's Colt cleared leather.

The .44-40 roared, and the revolutionary went down with a slug in his breastbone.

Mexicans numbers three and four dropped the crate they'd been carrying and made a dash for the safety of the warehouse, leaving number two standing there with a revolver in his hand and a look of stark terror on his face.

The terror was justified. The man was an armed adversary, and Longarm not only couldn't trust him, he couldn't even communicate with the guy to ask him to surrender. His options seemed to be limited. He triggered

163

two shots into the man's chest and face and took a moment to make sure the first one was down and dead. He was.

By then, the other pair were nearing the sanctuary of the bodega where the thick adobe walls would afford protection.

Longarm snapped two shots after them but succeeded only in lending even more speed to their headlong rush to safety.

Longarm could still see the backs of those two receding into the shadows when a puff of white smoke appeared beside the doorway. A moment later a large slug buried itself with a thud onto the adobe of the corral wall.

That made three inside or possibly more.

Longarm grabbed the 10 gauge and made a tactical withdrawal. Or maybe that was supposed to be called a strategic retreat. He couldn't remember which, but whatever the term—he got his ass behind cover. Briskly.

He leaned the shotgun against the wall—damned thing so far was more trouble than it was worth—and quickly reloaded the Colt.

While he was doing that his eyes rested absently on the crate Mexicans three and four had just dropped.

No wonder Jurneman would not want his business conducted in the open, Longarm saw.

The crate had broken open, and Longarm could see the polished brass and steel of a Gatling gun inside.

The second crate was slightly smaller. Longarm supposed that one would contain the tripod mount for the rapid-firing gun and perhaps some of the tall magazines that fed ammunition into the hopper that recharged each barrel as it came around in rotation.

As far as Longarm knew it was legal for any citizen to buy and sell Gatling guns. Including selling them to Mexican revolutionaries if he damn well pleased.

What folks on this side of the border might be expected

to protest, though, was the source of those guns: The crates bore markings indicating they were the property of the U.S. Army.

And selling Gatlings stolen from the army, well, that could get a boy into hot water.

No wonder Adolph hadn't wanted to be caught. And no wonder the insurrectionists on the other side wanted him free at least long enough to deliver these goods.

Four wagons waiting on the Mexican side of the river, Longarm thought. How many Gatling guns would it take to fill four wagons? And just what effect would that have toward making this revolution the next successful one?

A bullet thumped into the corral wall not far from where Longarm was crouching. Time enough to think about the picky little details of this mess later on, he realized. Right now he had a situation that needed taking care of.

He lifted the 10 gauge and propped the twin tubes on top of the corral gatepost. Dragged one hammer back—damned if he wanted to cock both of them and risk some mechanical malfunction that could touch both those huge barrels off at the same time—and aimed at the extreme left edge of the open warehouse doorway, which was the last place he'd seen gunsmoke.

The goose gun bellowed with a noise like that of a three-pounder field piece, and over at the bodega a significant chunk of framework disappeared in a cloud of dust and splinters.

Not bad, Longarm thought, as he thumbed back the second hammer and gave them another salute on the other side of the door opening.

He heard a scream but did not get excited about it. One of them could be trying to fool him into thinking there were fewer defenders than was the case.

"You son of a bitch," a voice carried to him across the corral floor. "Is that you, Long?"

"It's me, Adolph," Longarm shouted back.

"I'm gonna kill your ass, Long."

"Come right over here an' do it then, Adolph."

Jurneman seemed awfully chatty for a man who was pinned down inside a warehouse. Longarm was sure the guy was up to something. The question was what.

If there . . . oh. Longarm cut the speculation short, fairly certain he knew now what they were doing.

That warehouse had a back door ideally placed for sneaking goods out and across the river. Or, more likely, sneaking goods out of Mexico and into the U.S. without bothering with formalities and taxes and all that shit.

But the point now was that it would have more than just the back door. There was a front way in, too. Or a front way out.

And since Jurneman was pretty much elected to be the one to stand there talking to distract Longarm—the non-English speaking Mexicans wouldn't accomplish much in that direction—it stood to reason that one or both of the Mexicans were sneaking out the front and then around here to the back so they could get a clear shot without Longarm ever knowing they were there.

Nice try, he thought.

He pushed the goose gun forward on the gate post until he reached a balance point that allowed him to leave it lying there where Jurneman could see it.

"Come out and surrender, Adolph. You'll stand a fair trial. You have my word on that." He shouted it out nice and loud. Two could think in the same terms of distraction, after all.

With the shotgun there by the gate, Longarm dropped lower into a crouch and mentally tossed a coin to see which side of the corral he should tackle first. To his right won—it's a lot easier for a right-handed man to shoot around a corner if his cover is on the left—and he pussy-footed in that direction with the .44-40 Colt in hand.

He paused beside the corner to listen. Sure enough, he could hear gravel crunch very softly under boot soles as one of the Mexicans tried to get the drop on him.

Surprise, fucker! Longarm thought, as he leaned to the side a few inches, took aim and fired.

Halfway along the corral wall, Mexican number four threw his hands in the air and collapsed. He wasn't surrendering. He was dying. Longarm trigged another shot into him just to make sure, then slithered around the corner and peeked around to the gate where he'd just been.

"What's going on out there?" Jurneman shouted. "What'd you do, Long?"

Longarm did not bother to answer. He waited. And every few moments he would look toward the front of the warehouse. Just in case Mexican number three wised up and reversed his line of travel around the building.

Number three didn't think of that, however. After what seemed a long time, but probably was not, the brim of the guy's sombrero appeared at the far corner of the corral.

Longarm assumed the guy wanted to see if the hat drew fire, but that was giving the revolutionary hero more credit than was his due. Turned out the man was still wearing the hat. He wasn't being sneaky. He was being stupid.

As soon as he'd exposed half the side of his face, Longarm blew it off.

He was sure he'd made a hit. Half a second after he fired, there was a pale, reddish-pink mist in the air and what was left of the Mexican fell sideways onto the ground.

"Who shot?" Jurneman yelled. "What's going on?"

"It's just me," Longarm called back. "Just me and you, Adolph, all alone. D'you want to give yourself up now?"

"Go fuck yourself, Long."

"Anatomically improbable," Longarm shouted back, "and emotionally unsatisfying. No thank you." He'd heard Henry say that once. He kinda liked it.

"You won't get me, damn you. You'll never take me in." Jurneman's voice cracked when he made that final declaration.

"Fine. Come out an' face me man-to-man," Longarm challenged. "I'll give you a fair chance."

"Damn you, Long. Damn you!"

There was silence for a little while.

"Well?" Longarm shouted.

"Damn you." The words were faint this time.

And then Longarm heard the muffled report of another gunshot.

Shit! he thought.

Adolph Jurneman was right about that after all. Longarm really wasn't going to take him in. Because Adoph Jurneman already took himself out.

That wasn't the way Longarm planned it.

But it would do, dammit. It would do.

Chapter 38

"I expect that's it," Longarm said. "I've already sent a wire to Billy Vail bringing him up to date. I'll have to stay in town here until the coroner's inquest is held and I can get a death certificate to take back and file with the federal court in Denver. But apart from that, Carlton, I expect everything is wrapped up here."

"Gatlings," Carlton said. His voice wasn't back to normal yet, but it was stronger than it probably had any right to be so soon after major surgery.

"Twenty four of them," Longarm said, "and twenty crates of .45-70 ammunition to go with them."

"Somebody over on the other side of the border is going to be awfully unhappy about this," Carlton said.

"Anybody that stupid deserves t'be unhappy," Longarm said. "He coulda made things easy for himself if he'd just placed an order with the factory. It would've been legal."

"Somehow," Carlton said, "I doubt your man Jurneman mentioned that when he offered the merchandise."

"No, I expect not. Anita, the credit for all this goes to you. You're the one gave me the tip about the warehouse. And you were right, by the way. Those guns are very special." He touched her shoulder—kinda wished he could touch something else too, but she was Carlton's girl now—and added, "I wish there was some way I could pay you a reward for your help, but there's no paper out on Jurneman that I know about."

"It is of no importance, *senor*." She glanced down at Carlton, who was propped up with some pillows behind him now. "You have already given to me the greatest treasure."

"I asked her to marry me, Custis."

"Congratulations, Carlton. That's. . . ."

"She said no," Carlton interrupted. "Said she isn't fit to be a decent man's wife." Carlton's hand found Anita's, took it and squeezed. "But she said she'll move in with me for as long as I want. And that, I can tell you right now, will be for however many days I've got left."

"I'm happy for you, Carlton. For both of you." Longarm bent down and gave Anita a chaste kiss on the cheek. A wedding gift would not be appropriate, of course. But he thought he ought to do something for the couple. He would probably have the better part of a week in El Paso before he was done with the coroner and the inquest. He would think of something.

He bid them good-bye and walked down the street to Torres's cafe. It was coming onto dinnertime and he hadn't taken time for lunch yet. And besides, he needed to return Torres's goose gun. Not that he could figure out why such a blunderbuss should be called a goose gun when the damn thing kicked like a mule.

Ella Torres waited on him and insisted on plying him with all her own favorites from the kitchen, not all of which were Longarm's, but what the hell. She was a nice kid. And thanks to Carlton, a live one. That was good. It was also a fact he'd pointed out repeatedly to Ella and to both her parents. That did not matter. They wanted to treat Longarm like a hero anyway. What could he do but smile and let them?

He enjoyed his meal and stopped in for a drink or two, then went back to the hotel quite thoroughly satisfied.

"Marshal Long?" asked the hotel clerk.

"Yes, Gordon?"

"I hope . . . forgive me if I've done anything wrong . . . but under the circumstances . . ." the hotel clerk cleared his throat and glanced around to make sure no one else could overhear. "Your guest, sir. I thought . . . considering . . . it might be better if she did not wait in public."

"My guest?" Longarm repeated.

"The young woman," Gordon prompted.

"Oh, yes. I'd forgotten." That would be Zoe Everly. Without anything beneath her skirts. Right.

Gordon gave him a look as if to say that Longarm must be completely daft if a woman like that could slip his mind. "I allowed her to wait in your room, sir. I hope that is all right."

"Yes, Gordon. Thank you very much."

Longarm retrieved his key and went up the stairs to his room.

Zoe, he discovered, not only lacked undergarments by the time Longarm joined her, but also any sort of clothing. She lay sprawled quite fetchingly across the bedspread, naked as a peeled egg and looking just as tasty.

Chapter 39

Longarm hoped to hell there was nobody in either of the adjoining rooms because Zoe was braying like a donkey in heat. All Longarm had to do was hold still while Zoe bucked and thumped and threw herself around with more than enough zest for the both of them.

And this was after he'd already taken the edge off her passion with the first fuck. The girl was . . . vigorous.

Not that he was complaining.

"Slow down, baby, or I'll cum too soon. That's it. That's better. Nice and . . . oh, yes. That's good."

He grabbed hold of her waist and hung on for the ride.

Zoe was on top at the moment, her hips churning fit to turn his juice into butter, her tits flapping and her head thrown back, her neck and throat corded with effort as she threw herself into her performance.

Sweat beaded under her tits and rolled from her armpits down her ribs and onto Longarm's hands.

She began the low, keening, wordless song that Longarm had come to know was Zoe's prelude to a climax. He took the hint and began to drive his hips upward to meet her downstrokes, impaling her all the harder on his shaft. She began to tremble and then quiver uncontrollably.

Finally with a piercing cry she reached her limits and exploded. Longarm could feel the contractions of her pussy when she came, and the sensation was enough to send him over the edge also. His fluids filled her and rolled out again, covering his balls and matting his pubic hair.

Zoe stopped dead still, held her position there above him and then collapsed.

He thought for a moment she was merely resting.

Truth was, she'd passed out.

Women did that sometimes, of course, and it never seemed to hurt them. Longarm considered it a compliment of sorts and figured he could just lie there and wait for her to come around again although he would have enjoyed a smoke while he waited for the yen to return.

She was unconscious for not more than ten or fifteen seconds before she awoke. Stretched. Smiled and kissed him.

"Give me a minute to catch my breath, sweetie. Then I'll lick all that lovely stuff off you and see if we can get the soldier to stand at attention again."

"Mmm. Bet he does."

Zoe yawned and relaxed.

Without warning, she became suddenly rigid as a slab of pine and after a few shocked seconds began to scream.

Longarm followed the direction of her frightened look and realized that she had good reason for her concern.

Ignacio Fernandez was standing in the now open door to Longarm's room.

Chapter 40

Fernandez clicked his heels together and bowed. The soldier was indeed standing to attention. Except it was the wrong soldier. And, anyway, Ignacio was no longer a soldier, desertion being frowned upon in most armies.

"I congratulate you, *senor*." Ignacio was having trouble taking his eyes off Zoe's tits. Longarm could sympathize with the problem.

"On my victory this afternoon?" Longarm asked. "Hush, dear," he said to Zoe, taking her by the shoulder and shaking her just a little to get her attention. After a moment she shut up and buried her face in Longarm's armpit, as if that would allow her to hide from the intruder.

"No, *senor*. On your conquest this evening."

"Yes, well, a fellow gets lucky sometimes. Would you roll off me, dear. Yeah, over on this side. Excuse us for a minute here, Captain."

"But of course, *senor*." Fernandez did not, however, avert his eyes as Longarm gently rolled Zoe off onto the side of the bed away from the door and pulled the sheet up over her.

Fernandez sighed when he did that.

Longarm sat on the side of the bed and reached for his cheroots and matches. "Care for a cigar?"

"No, thank you."

"I, uh, assume you had a reason for this . . . visit?"

Fernandez looked startled. "Oh! Yes. Of course."

Longarm bit the tip off a cheroot, struck a match and lighted it. The smoke didn't taste quite as good as it might have. He eyed the pistol in Nacho's belt and considered the exact movement he would require to snatch his Colt out of the holster he'd hung on the bedpost, thought about precisely where he should aim to best incapacitate the now former officer.

"My patron is, shall we say, unhappy with you, *senor.*"

"Is that a fact? Sure you don't want one of these smokes? They're pretty good."

"My patron has asked me to deliver to you a message, *senor*. An invitation, if you will."

"An invitation."

"Exactly, *senor*. My patron now will not receive the articles he already paid for. This is your fault."

"Already paid for? That wasn't very smart of him, Captain."

Fernandez scowled. "Partly paid for. Do not quibble."

"Sorry." Zoe had been trembling so hard Longarm could feel the bed shaking. Now she was calming down. He was glad for that.

"My patron issues to you a challenge. To the duel, *senor*. My patron would meet you *mano a mano*. One to one, yes? Only the two of you and may the better man live."

"I believe you said it was an invitation. What if I decline?"

Fernandez looked apologetic. A little bit anyway. "The invitation is not to be rejected, *senor*. Men would be hired. They would seek you. They would also seek out your friends. We know who they are, *senor*. You would not be able to defend them forever. They would die. If you accept the invitation...," Fernandez smiled, "only you need die."

"Or live," Longarm said. He inhaled some of the excellent smoke, then blew a series of smoke rings toward the ceiling.

"My patron awaits your response, *senor*."

"Mind telling me who this patron of yours is, Captain?"

"His name would mean nothing to you."

"Uh huh. And what are the details of this invite?"

"I am sure you remember the place where the merchandise belonging to the movement was stored."

"Yeah, I expect that I do."

"At that place, *senor*. In the corral. Half an hour past the dawn."

"What about seconds?"

"You may bring one only. As will the patron." Fernandez stiffened to attention again. "I shall have that honor myself, *senor*."

Longarm nodded. "All right then, Captain. At the warehouse, half hour past dawn."

"My patron will be pleased to learn of your response, *senor*." Fernandez clicked his heels again, and his hand started upward as if to salute. He remember the error in time and brought his hand back down to his side. "Tomorrow, *senor*. And now I bid you a... pleasant good night." He laughed a little and left.

"Shit," Longarm said. "Reckon I forgot t' bolt that door, didn't I?"

Zoe crawled out from beneath the sheet and hugged him.

And if she wanted to give him succor thinking this could be his last night on earth, who was he to deny her the pleasure?

Chapter 41

Tendrils of morning mist still lingered on the surface of the placid Rio Grande when Longarm disembarked from his cab a good quarter mile away from the bodega and walked the rest of the distance. He felt good. He'd slept well, body sated and empty. Now his belly was still full and warm from an excellent breakfast. He felt loose and fit.

He would have liked to show up at the warehouse with a company of Texas Rangers or a phalanx of police to surround the place and resolve the problem the easy way. Unfortunately, he still didn't have any Rangers handy to back him up, and he knew better than to ask the El Paso police for assistance. They were more apt to show up, all right. And then arrest him for littering if he dropped any spent cartridge cases onto the ground.

He especially would have liked to have Carlton there to back him. That wasn't possible, of course. But the good news was that in a few months it just damned well might be. Carlton was on the mend and even Jim Quayne said now that he expected a full recovery.

Quayne was also more excited than ever about the paper he would write for the medical journals outlining Anita's methods of wound treatment. That information could save a good many lives in years to come, Jim claimed.

Longarm finished the cheroot he'd lighted on the way out from town, then tossed the butt aside as he reached the back of the corral.

There were two horses tied outside the enclosure, he saw. Deliberately, of course, to assure him that only Fernandez and his mysterious patron were present.

That might even be so, Longarm thought.

Or not.

In either case he didn't see that he had much choice about it. He could defend himself just fine, he figured. But Carlton wouldn't be able to handle a gunfight for months at best. And Anita would have no defense at all if somebody wanted to hire her dead.

"Good morning, Captain."

"Good morning, *senor*. May I inquire where is your second?"

"Don't have one," Longarm said. Which was the truth. The only man he would have trusted would have been Carlton Mitchell, and that wasn't going to happen. "Where's your patron?"

Fernandez went to the gate and looked outside in both directions before he came back into the corral and walked to the back door of the warehouse. He said something in Spanish, and a haughty don stepped into view.

"Well, I'll be damned," Longarm said. "Good morning, *Senor* Figaroa."

Fernandez was taken aback. Joaquin Figaroa was not. He held himself rigidly erect, a large leather case carried in both hands as if they were an offering to some sort of pagan god.

"It is an honor to face someone of your reputation, *senor*," Figaroa said. "I look forward to this. And with your permission, *senor*, I have brought the foils for our use."

Figaroa handed the case to Fernandez, then unlatched the lid and opened it. A pair of slender fencing swords rested in carefully-fitted, velvet-lined pockets inside the presentation case. Their hilts were polished steel or perhaps German silver with gold wire inlays. The hand guards were ornately decorated. And there were no safety buttons in place on the tips as would have been the case had these foils been intended for recreational fencing.

"Very nice, *senor*," Longarm said.

"Thank you. You may, of course, have your choice between them."

"That's nice o' you I'm sure, but if I understand this correctly, *Senor* Figaroa, the choice o' weapons belongs to the challenged party. Namely me. Not to the challenger. Namely you. So I reckon we won't be needing these fine swords o' yours because that's not what I choose for the weapons."

"But . . . but . . ."

"The choice is mine, *senor*. I choose Colt's revolvers at twenty paces."

"That is barbaric, *senor*."

"Not at all. Wouldn't be fair to you if we was to draw and fire, I agree," Longarm said. "So we'll do 'er just like we had proper dueling pistols. Weapons in hand. Back-to-back. Walk out ten paces each. Turn an' fire on Captain Fernandez's command. I reckon that should satisfy anybody that this will be a fair and proper duel, wouldn't you say?"

"But I . . ."

"If you want t' back water, *senor*, an' withdraw your challenge, I expect that'd be your privilege."

The insult was slightly veiled. But it was for damned sure an insult. Figaroa recoiled as if he'd just been struck in the face. And by his lights, probably he had. "I accept your terms, *senor*," he said stiffly.

"Very well, *senor*. You got a belly gun?"

Figaroa quite obviously did not like the crudity of the reference. But he pretty much had to accept it at this point. He turned to Nacho and snapped, "Your pistol, *senor*."

"Si, patron," Fernandez handed over his revolver. It was one of the large-bore Smith and Wesson's, not a Colt, but Longarm wasn't going to quibble over that small discrepancy.

"Since I have no second," Longarm said, "we'll let the captain here attend to the details."

Figaroa nodded.

Nacho positioned them in the center of the dusty corral. The sun was well over the horizon now and was slanting gold and bright at an acute angle. To his credit, Nacho placed the combatants fair and square so neither one of them would be facing into the morning sunlight.

"I shall count in English," he announced. "You will each step forward on each count. At the distance of the tenth count you will stop. I will tell you to cock your pieces. I will warn you of the command to come. Then, when I say 'turn' you will each be free to turn and to fire. Is this understood?"

"Si."

"Sure is."

"Prepare, please."

They stood back to back. Longarm yawned. It wasn't disinterest actually. It was tension. He pulled the big Colt from his holster and held it with his elbow cocked, hand and gun muzzle pointing upward.

"At the ready, if you please. On my instruction now. One . . . two. . . ."

At the count of ten Longarm stopped and waited.

A bullet sizzled past his left ear and almost at that same moment he heard the roar of the gunshot.

The betrayal was not entirely unexpected. And if Figaroa wanted to break the rules of the Code *Duelo*, fuck him.

Longarm spun, dropping into a crouch as he did so.

The big Colt was barking even before he'd completed the turn.

Fernandez looked sadly down at the body of his patron. "I am sorry, *senor*."

"Not your fault, Captain. I don't hold it against you that he didn't have nerve enough t' face a man."

"But, *senor*. That is not why I give my apology."

"Something else I don't know about, Nacho?"

"Sadly, *senor*, I must confess that this is so." Fernandez turned and barked a command in Spanish, and a dozen revolutionaries armed with rifles came rushing out of the warehouse.

"Shit," Longarm grumbled. And shot Nacho Fernandez in the belly.

That was probably all he would have time for, he figured, but he wanted to make sure that job got done regardless.

Fernandez went down, and Longarm shot him again in the side of the head from a distance of only two feet or so. The man's head exploded into a red jelly mixed with globs of gray ooze.

Beyond the dead man, Longarm heard the sharp, rolling crackle of gunfire.

He flinched, bracing himself for the hammer blows that would put him down, too.

Inexplicably he felt . . . nothing. Not even the impact of a first bullet. Was this what death felt like? If so, why could he still smell the gunsmoke and hear the continued firing?

He looked up in time to see the last of Figaroa's insurrectionists crumple into the dirt.

Lining the corral walls there were others who seemed to be enjoying a turkey shoot with the Mexicans as the focus of their fun.

The shooters—Americans, he saw, but a rough-looking crowd of thugs—finished what they were doing and disappeared from sight.

By the time Longarm got outside the corral to talk to them, they had dispersed and were on their way back to town with a good lead over him.

He never got to say a word to any on them.

"It was you, wasn't it?" Longarm said. The words were accusatory but the tone of voice was not.

"I do not know what you mean, Marshal," T. Wade Kaufman said, his expression bland. "And I hope you will keep in mind that I said that."

"Sure. But I still say it was you."

"If we can look at this hypothetically, Marshal, one might say that an . . . informant"—. Kaufman couldn't avoid smiling a little at that one, what with Zoe Everly working in his own office daily—"an informant could have mentioned the planned events to an, um, interested party."

"Uh huh."

"And this interested party, if such a person were to exist, might well have had self interest involved here. Matters of, oh, let's pretend there could be matters of commerce involved that would have been disrupted if a new regime were to flower in Chihuahua."

"I'm still with you."

Kaufman spread his hands. "But that is all hypothetical, of course."

"Yeah," Longarm said. "Strictly what-if and make-believe."

"Exactly." Kaufman beamed.

"If . . . not that I'm sayin' it's so . . . but if there was such an interested party, then I reckon I'd have t' thank him."

"If there were such a person," Kaufman said, "he probably would tell you that you are welcome. And admit to self-interest lest you think he was going soft."

"No," Longarm said with a grin. "I don't reckon I would think that of him at all."

"Very well then. Is there anything else, Marshal? I am a very busy man and haven't time for any more hypothetical situations."

"No. There's nothing else." Longarm crossed the room, then paused at the door. He grinned at the fat lawyer. "Thanks, Wade."

Kaufman scowled at him.

On his way out to visit with Carlton and Anita, Longarm paused at the reception desk only long enough to deliver a whispered message. "Tonight again. An' come hungry. We're gonna have the finest El Paso has to offer delivered up t' the room, hear."

Zoe acted as if she hadn't heard.

Longarm was whistling as he strolled down the street in the direction of Jim Quayne's office.

Watch for

LONGARM AND THE LADY LAWYER

281st novel in the exciting LONGARM series
from Jove

Coming in April!

LONGARM

**Explore the exciting Old West with one
of the men who made it wild!**

JAKE LOGAN
TODAY'S HOTTEST ACTION WESTERN!

APR 3 0 2010